the jungle around us

FLANNERY
O'CONNOR
AWARD
FOR
SHORT
FICTION

Nancy Zafris,
Series Editor

STORIES BY

anne raeff

THE UNIVERSITY OF
GEORGIA PRESS
athens

Athens, Georgia 30602
www.ugapress.org

Designed by Kaelin Chappell Broaddus
Set in 10/14 Quadraat Regular
Printed and bound by Sheridan Books, Inc.

The paper in this book meets the guidelines for
permanence and durability of the Committee on
Production Guidelines for Book Longevity of
the Council on Library Resources.

Most University of Georgia Press titles are
available from popular e-book vendors.

Printed in the United States of America
16 17 18 19 20 c 5 4 3 2 1

Library of Congress Cataloging-in-Publication Data
Names: Raeff, Anne, 1959–   author.
Title: The jungle around us : stories / by Anne Raeff.
Description: First edition. | Athens : The University of Georgia Press, [2016]
Identifiers: LCCN 2015047531| ISBN 9780820349893 (hardcover :
acid-free paper) | ISBN 9780820349909 (ebook)
Classification: LCC PS3618.A36 A6 2016 | DDC 813/.6—dc23
LC record available at http://lccn.loc.gov/2015047531

To my mother, Lillian Raeff,
and in memory of my grandparents
Drs. Irving and Josephine (Pepa) Gottesman,
all of whom briefly made their home in the jungle.

And to my sister, Catherine Raeff, my first reader.

CONTENTS

ACKNOWLEDGMENTS

I am honored to be among the winners of the Flannery O'Connor Award and would like to thank Nancy Zafris, the series editor, for choosing my collection and for her support of my writing and of these stories. I am also grateful to the team at the University of Georgia Press for all their hard work throughout the publication process. Thank you, also, to Sheryl Johnston, my amazing publicist, for helping me get the book out into the world.

I would also like to acknowledge literary journals in general for all they do to keep the short story alive. I would especially like to thank Carolyn Kuebler and Stephen Donadio at *New England Review* for their continued support of my work over the years; Christine Sneed for choosing "Carlito on Pink" for the *Fifth Wednesday Journal*, which she guest-edited; Robert Fogarty of *Antioch Review*; and Meakin Armstrong at *Guernica* for his support.

I would never have written a word without my family, friends, and students. They have given me not only support and inspiration but the messy challenges of human interaction, without which there would be no stories. And finally, thank you, Lori

Ostlund, my wife, for the adventures and for the ten thousand miles and for absolutely everything.

Some of the stories in this collection were published previously.

- "Carlito on Pink" appeared in *Fifth Wednesday Journal* 13 (Fall 2013).
- "Keeping an Eye on Jakobson" appeared in *New England Review* 32, no. 3 (2011).
- "The Doctors' Daughter" appeared in *Guernica*, February 2012.
- "The Buchovskys on Their Own" appeared in *New England Review* 26, no. 2 (2005).
- "After the War" appeared in *Oasis*, 1996.
- "A Letter" appeared in *Side Show*, 1995.
- "Sonya's Mood" appeared in *Side Show*, 1996.
- "Maximiliano" appeared in *Antioch Review*, 2016.
- "Chinese Opera" appeared in *New England Review*, 2016.

My thanks to the original publishers for selecting my work.

the jungle
around us

the doctors' daughter

"Don't forget to feed the chickens," Pepa's parents told her when they left for the jungle to take care of the yellow-fever victims. As if she could forget such a thing. Wasn't she the one who took care of them, who collected the eggs, swept up the droppings, slit their throats with the scalpel her father had given her for this very purpose? If she had forgotten to feed the chickens, they would have come pecking at the back door, would have jumped onto the kitchen windowsill and poked their beaks between the louvers. How could she possibly forget to feed the chickens?

The chickens had been Pepa's idea, after all. Her parents had not approved at first. "What do we know about keeping chickens?" they said. But they seemed to forget that in the beginning they had not known any of it. They had not known how to cook beans, had not known the taste of fried bananas or the Spanish word for rice, had not known how to hang mosquito netting or the sound of monkeys screaming in the night or that you had to bribe the health inspectors as well as hide the water cistern when they came around every so often looking for what they called "standing water."

"What do they expect us to do, live without water?" her father had asked when the inspectors threatened to turn the cistern upside down.

Pepa smiled and spoke to the inspectors, using the few words of Spanish she knew. "Please," she said, "can I offer you some coffee?" When she served them the coffee in the porcelain cups they had brought with them from Vienna, she set a few coins in each saucer. The inspectors thanked her profusely for the coffee, which they said was the best they had ever had. They even bowed as they left, and Pepa's father smiled and bowed, also. After that, the inspectors were her responsibility too, like the chickens.

"I will learn how to take care of chickens," Pepa told them, and she did. She bargained hard for them at the market, and she and her brother Kurt carried them home upside down by their legs the way the market woman had shown them.

When her parents left for the jungle to care for the victims of the yellow-fever epidemic, they did not know how long they would be gone. Their friend the pharmacist had offered to take Pepa and Kurt while they were away, but they did not accept his offer. At fourteen Pepa was old enough to handle the house, to watch after her brother.

"But won't they be afraid to stay in the house alone?" the pharmacist had asked. It was Sunday afternoon and, as they did every Sunday, they were dining with the pharmacist.

"They will not be afraid," Pepa's father had said very sternly. "We will not be afraid again," he added. "Right?" he asked, turning to Pepa.

"I am not afraid," she replied.

"If they need anything, anything at all, I am here," the pharmacist said.

On the evening of the first day of her parents' absence, the pharmacist knocked on the door. She and Kurt were doing their lessons, their books spread out on the dining room table. Pepa prepared coffee and brought it to the table.

"Your parents are very brave to go to the jungle," the pharmacist said.

"It is their duty as doctors to help people," Pepa told him.

"But it is very dangerous," the pharmacist said.

"Life is dangerous," Pepa replied.

"I suppose it is," the pharmacist said, laughing. "Well, promise you will let me know if you need something."

"I promise," Pepa said, but she could not imagine what she could possibly need that the pharmacist had.

For two weeks her parents were gone, and during this time Pepa took care of her brother as she did when they were not in the jungle. She prepared meals. She went to the market and mopped the floors and fed the chickens, of course. She made sure that Kurt took a bath every day, and she helped him with his lessons. When her parents returned from the jungle, their clothes caked in red mud, their breaths smelling of hunger, Pepa washed their clothes, stomping and rinsing them over and over, the water flowing red like blood. Then she made them a twelve-egg omelet, for the protein, and fed them mounds of rice and fried bananas. After the meal, which they ate dutifully and in silence, they slept for twenty-four hours straight.

It was after they returned from the yellow-fever epidemic that her parents began sleeping in the clinic. Their clinic was on the other side of the patio—two small rooms that smelled of rubbing alcohol and bleach that they had painted a soothing blue like the eyes of an Alaskan husky, like winter. The house, they said, had a strange odor, something sweet that kept them up at night, gave them headaches. Pepa understood, however, that it was not about the smell. Rather, at night, when there was time to think, to remember their careers at the best hospital in Vienna, they needed not a soft mattress to lie upon or the sound of their children breathing in the next room but the certainty of steel instruments and the clean smell of alcohol. "We are just on the other side of the patio if you need us," her father said every night before they retired to the clinic.

"I am not afraid," Pepa said.

In fact, she could not imagine what could happen to Kurt and her as they slept. They were far from the dangers of Europe now, as far as one could be. At night they kept the louvers open just a crack, just enough to let the breeze in and keep the monkeys out. The monkeys were the only danger. They could destroy the house in a few minutes—pull all the dishes from the shelves, smash them on the cool tile floor, rip the sheets from the bed, urinate on the walls.

In the market, the cabbage woman did not even know there was a war on. "What are they fighting about?" she asked Pepa, and Pepa did not know how to answer her.

"They are fighting over Europe," she said, and the woman smiled.

"They will regret it in the end," the woman said. "They always do."

At night, after Kurt had gone to sleep, she lay in her dark room listening to the sounds of the night, to the insects, the monkeys, the rain. She imagined her parents lying on the jungle floor burning up with fever, clutching at the red earth, gasping for breath. She made herself look into their wide-open dead eyes. She lay there perfectly still, arms at her side, palms up, her heart beating slowly as if she were asleep. She would never be afraid again. That was what she learned when her parents went to where the yellow fever was.

After her parents' return from the jungle, Pepa began going out at night. She walked all the way to the edge of town, to where the jungle began. She walked into the jungle, pulling branches apart as she went. Each time she went farther and farther, but always she found her way out. She could sense the path, sense which branches she had touched before, and, always, she found herself back out on the dirt path that led to the town, to the whitewashed houses, to the plaza, the church. When she had mastered the jungle and no longer thought about the possibility of getting lost in its rubbery shadows, she began spending her evenings, after she had finished her lessons, on the church steps. On Friday and Saturday nights there was a *banda* and people danced, and Pepa watched, counting the steps, counting the beats. Gradually she moved from her position on the steps closer and closer to the dancers. Every night she came a little closer until she stood among the young women who were waiting to be asked to dance, and on the second night, a somber young man approached her. "I am Guillermo and you are the doctors' daughter, no?"

"Yes," she said, and he led her to where the people were dancing.

That first night they did not speak again until after the *banda* stopped playing. Pepa concentrated on the music and on Guillermo's hand pressed against her back. When the members of the *banda* had put away their instruments and the dancers had dispersed, Guillermo wanted to walk her home, but Pepa said that she liked walking by herself.

"You are not afraid?" he asked.

"Are you afraid?" she asked.

"No, of course not," he said.

"You see, there is nothing to be afraid of," she said, and she began walking across the plaza toward her house. That is how it started with Guillermo.

The next night Guillermo was waiting for her. "I thought you wouldn't come tonight," he said.

"Why did you think that?" she asked.

"I thought you were angry because I said that you might be afraid," he explained.

"That is no reason to be angry," Pepa said, and the music started, and Pepa took his hand and led him to where the other dancers were, and after the dancing was over they walked to the edge of the town, to where the jungle started, and Pepa led him into the thickness of the jungle. "Close your eyes," she said. "It is better to feel the way than to try to see." So he closed his eyes and took her hand. Around them was the sound of millions of insects. After a while they stopped and the sound of the insects grew louder like applause or water plunging onto rock. Guillermo kissed her and she was not afraid of his tongue and his hands on her body, and she wanted to stay with him all night, wanted to lie down on the wet earth, but he turned around and began walking back, pulling her behind him, and soon they were out on the road and the sound of the insects grew distant, and the trees no longer protected them from the stars. "Don't look up. The stars will blind you," Pepa said, and Guillermo laughed, but he did not look up.

Pepa's parents did not notice a change in her. They tended to their patients and ate the food that Pepa cooked for them with their usual lack of gusto. They did not notice that Pepa swayed gently back and forth while she washed the dishes because they were too focused on the end of the war. Their visas would be going through, and soon they would be able to leave. They practiced the few English words they knew. "Hello, how are you?" they were always saying. "I am fine, thank you, and you?" During dinner they practiced their numbers, chanting them as if they were a victory cheer. Pepa tried to close her ears to all of it and concentrated instead on Guillermo's hands on the soft insides of her thighs.

It was only after their visas arrived that she told her parents that she and Guillermo were expecting a child. Her parents did not say a word. They looked her in the eyes and shook their heads, and Pepa ran to her room and flung herself on the bed, but she did not cry. They did not come to her. She heard them talking softly, still sitting at the table where she had left them. All night she waited for them to get up from the table, to go out to the clinic so she could go to Guillermo. He would know what to do. They could work on the coffee plantations. But always when she awoke, she could hear her parents at the table, talking softly, and their talking worked like hypnosis, lulling her back to sleep.

In the morning, her parents came into her room, spoke to her from the doorway. "Pepa," they called. How had she slept so long, so late? She always woke before dawn, when the roosters crowed. The chickens. She had forgotten the chickens. Her mother followed her out of the house onto the patio. "Where are you going?"

"To feed the chickens," Pepa said.

"I already did it," her mother said, putting her hand on her shoulder, leading her back into the house.

Again she thought about going to Guillermo. Her parents would not have run after her. It was not their way. But she hadn't gone to him. She couldn't, so she slept.

The talking continued. Sometimes their voices were loud and angry and at other times she thought she heard them crying, but she could not find the strength to get out of bed to open the door just a crack, to stand by the door and listen. How would they manage in New York without her, she wondered. Who would take care of Kurt? Who would make sure there was always a meal on the table? It did not occur to her that in New York there were no health inspectors to fool, no chickens to raise. In New York, she and her brother would go to school, and they would have to concentrate on their studies. Yes, she would rest, simply rest. There was still time, just a little time, to remember how she and Guillermo had danced like ships and lain down on the jungle floor.

In the clinic, her parents prepared the table, the instruments. When they came to get her they said, "Come," and they both held out their hands and the three of them walked slowly to the clinic, where her mother helped her up onto the examination table. She saw the instruments then, lined up like soldiers, and everything smelled so clean.

keeping an eye on jakobson

When Simone and Juliet came home from school, Jakobson was sitting in the backyard smoking one of his big, smelly cigars. As usual, his hair was unkempt and he had ashes all over his suit jacket and in his beard. Things were always a little upside down with Jakobson. He did not visit often, but when he did they always sat in the backyard because Jakobson could not tolerate an afternoon or evening without his cigars, and their father, who suffered from asthma, could not tolerate being in an enclosed space with Jakobson's cigars. When Jakobson visited, they even ate in the backyard, something they did not do on any other occasion.

Their father never called Jakobson—which was pronounced with a soft *j* like a *y*—by his first name as he did his other friends. "Doesn't Jakobson have a first name?" they asked their father.

"Of course he does," he answered.

"Then why do you call him by just his last name?"

"Because our professor used to call us all by our last names."

"But he doesn't call you Buchovsky," they pointed out.

"He used to."

"Why did he stop?"

"I'm not sure. He just did," their father said.

Their father had met Jakobson in graduate school; now, they were colleagues in the history department at Columbia, where their father taught courses in Russian imperial history. Jakobson's field was the Soviet period, and despite the fact that Jakobson still had what their father called "a naive soft spot for the ideals of communism," they had remained friends all these years.

Juliet and Simone were surprised to find Jakobson sitting in the garden because their father had not mentioned anything about Jakobson coming, and he always told them when they were receiving visitors. There were always preparations the night before—shopping to be done, lamb to be marinated. When Jakobson came, they always had *shashlik* because their father considered it an outdoor food even though he did not barbecue it outdoors but broiled it inside under the broiler. Barbecues, he said, were superfluous. A broiler was so much less trouble.

"Are they teaching you about the war?" Jakobson asked Simone and Juliet before they could even say hello properly. He pulled hard, not pensively the way he usually did, on his long, scraggly beard.

"Which war?" Simone asked because there were so many of them.

"Which war?" Jakobson stood up and raised his fist in the air. The ashes flew from his clothes, and Simone watched them fall back down to the ground. "Which war?" he repeated, beating the air with his fist.

"He means the Vietnam War," their father said calmly.

"On Fridays we have to bring in articles from the newspaper. The teacher puts them all on a bulletin board called *The State of the World*," Simone said.

"And then what?" Jakobson sat down again and was suddenly limp, slumped back in his chair.

"Nothing. Sometimes she asks us to tell the class what our articles are about, but usually she just staples them to the bulletin board so we can read them at our own leisure if we finish our work or get to school early."

"All the girls in my class have POW bracelets," Simone added. "I don't have one because my father says it's a money-making scheme." Just last week had been the week of the POW bracelet. Simone had bought one with her own money and proudly shown it to her father the minute he came home. Her POW, Private Kenneth F. Snelling, was from Wisconsin. He was a big fan of the Twins baseball team, played the trumpet, and was very handy. "I had to fill out a special registration form so when he's released he'll know that I have been wearing his bracelet and he'll write me a letter," Simone had announced proudly to her father.

"Do you have any idea what the prisoner-of-war camps are like?" her father had asked.

Perhaps because their father did not believe in television and thus did not have one, Simone imagined the POW camps in Vietnam to be like the POW camp in Arizona, where her father had been stationed during World War II. She pictured Kenneth F. Snelling eating ice cream and cutting down trees, only the trees were in a jungle because she knew that in Vietnam there were jungles and lots of rain and wide, muddy rivers, but she did not tell her father that. Instead she shook her head because she knew, from the way he had led her to the table and sat down right across from her and looked straight into her eyes, that her vision was incorrect. "These bracelets," he said, holding the bracelet up for her to see as if he were giving a demonstration about an onion peeler or apple corer, "are nothing more than war profiteering. Someone sitting at home in a nice cozy house is making money off of this young man's suffering, not to mention the suffering of an entire country." Their father never raised his voice, and he did not raise his voice when he delivered these words either. He spoke steadily and calmly, and when he was finished, he hugged Simone and she gave him the bracelet and the photo and the little description of Kenneth F. Snelling, and they drove down to Krolick's and returned it. They did not explain to Mrs. Krolick why they were returning it, and she did not protest. On the way home Simone's wrist felt empty. She had wanted to show Kenneth's photograph to the other girls in her fifth-grade class. She had already started thinking of him as Kenneth.

Actually Juliet and Simone did know some things about the war—they knew about the communists and the Viet Cong and they knew about napalm. They knew that their father did not like communism because it was, like religion, a fantasy that led people to commit horrible acts of violence. They knew also that he thought the war in Vietnam was misguided. "You can't kill an idea," he told them. "You just have to be patient and wait until it dies." Simone and Juliet even knew two people who were fighting in Vietnam—one of the McSwene boys who lived next door and Mrs. Tuttle's son. They didn't actually know Mrs. Tuttle's son. They knew Mrs. Tuttle and that her son was in Vietnam, but they did not tell Jakobson what they knew because he was crying.

"Come, come, Jakobson," their father said. He asked Simone to go inside to make Jakobson a bourbon on the rocks. "Lots of bourbon," her father called after her. Simone brought out the bourbon and handed it to Jakobson, who drank it in one gulp. Then he dropped the hand that held the glass limply to his side. Simone was sure he was going to let the glass fall and that it would shatter on the bricks, but he held on to it.

"Should I get another one?" she asked her father.

"Not just yet," he said.

Jakobson was still crying.

Their father was telling Jakobson that as soon as the Columbia riots had started, he should have packed up his books and notes and gone home like he had. "They're young, Jakobson," their father said. "They don't think things through."

"Then, Isaac, we have failed. It is our job to teach them to think things through!" Jakobson stood up again.

Juliet was twirling her hair, watching some birds in the apple tree, doing her best not to stare at Jakobson.

"Later they will realize that you are not the enemy, but now we have to lie low."

"Lie low! You mean run away. That is cowardice!"

"No, Jakobson, it is reason."

"If you had seen them, but of course you didn't because you had already fled. If they had had guns, they would have killed me. You didn't see their faces when they barged in on me."

"Jakobson, calm down. You're exaggerating. They know you. They know you are on their side."

"You did not see their faces."

"No, but you will see. Next year they will sit in your class and take notes and ask you questions."

"I will never go back there! Not after what they have done. You cannot imagine, Isaac, what it feels like to see your life's work go up in flames like . . . like . . . the Great Library of Alexandria." This time his fist shot up, and then he slumped back in his chair. Then he shot his fist up again. "Traitors!" he screamed. "Traitors! Traitors! Traitors!"

Isaac put his hand gently on Jakobson's shoulder, but Jakobson kept screaming, "Traitors! Traitors! Traitors!" Juliet and Simone sat properly in their chairs, not looking right at him but not looking away either because they had been taught that it was rude not to look people in the eye when they were talking. Their father patted Jakobson a few more times on the shoulder, but he did not stop screaming, so their father changed his position, walking calmly over to where Simone and Juliet were sitting stiffly in their green plastic garden chairs, neither staring nor looking away, neither frowning nor smiling. Their father crouched down behind them, put one hand on each of their shoulders and whispered, "All my life and all my dreams are hanging from this apple tree."

This line, which was one of their father's favorites, came from *Max und Moritz*, an old comic book from his childhood that chronicled the adventures of two mischievous and often malicious boys. The line was taken from a particularly malicious scene in which Max and Moritz were standing on a rooftop and laughing hysterically as they looked down at an old woman who had just discovered their latest prank—her beloved chickens hanging from her apple tree. Covering her eyes with her hands, the woman cried out, "All my life and all my dreams hang from this apple tree." Simone and Juliet did not laugh even though they knew their father had wanted to add some levity to the situation. Somehow, this line from *Max und Moritz* of which he was so fond never made them laugh, although he used it time and time again when he accused them of what he called *overreacting*, like the time Simone cried and cried when her perfectly-broken-in baseball mitt got ruined because she left out in the rain.

Their father stood up again and went back to Jakobson. "Come on now, Jakobson, it's not the end of the world," he said, but Jakobson still kept screaming. Tomorrow, Simone thought, he will have a terrible sore throat. After a while, their father threw up his hands. "Don't you have homework to do, girls?" he asked.

"Of course we have homework," Juliet said.

"You might as well get to it, then," their father said almost sadly, as if he did not really want them to leave.

After they finished their homework, which did not take very long as they had both managed to do most of it at school during lunch, they sat in the living room at the edge of the couch until

Jakobson finally stopped screaming, and then they went outside again to ask their father for permission to ride their bicycles.

"Be home before dusk," he told them as he always did because, according to him, dusk was the most dangerous time to be riding a bicycle. "The light is deceptive," their father always told them. "It is safer to be out on the roads at night because people are more careful, but dusk gives them a false sense of confidence," he explained almost every time they went off on their bicycles.

"Don't worry," they said, and their father said that he wouldn't worry if they were home before dusk.

They rode their bicycles to the park and watched some people play tennis. Juliet wanted to go to Krolick's to get a Mounds bar, but Krolick's reminded Simone of Kenneth, so they went to the stationery store instead. The man at the stationery store gave them each a piece of bubble gum in addition to the Mounds bars.

"Why do we always go to Krolick's when he's so much nicer?" Simone asked Juliet when they were back outside unlocking their bicycles.

"It smells funny in there," Juliet said.

"I like the smell. It smells like those boxes in the basement full of Dad's notes and old letters."

"I guess I don't like that smell," Juliet said.

"Well I do," Simone said.

They went back to the park to eat their chocolate, and then it was time to head home. They pedaled as fast as they could uphill, standing up on their bicycles so they wouldn't have to get off and walk. They had a rule about staying on their bikes no matter how hard it was and no matter how slowly they had to go.

At home things were quieter. Jakobson was taking a nap on the couch in their father's study, and their father was making dinner. "Don't make a ruckus when you go upstairs," he told them. Jakobson slept through dinner, and when it was time for Juliet and Simone to go to bed, he was still sleeping. In the morning, they all ate breakfast together outside. Jakobson wasn't crying anymore, and he ate his breakfast and drank his coffee without saying a word.

"Make sure you come home right after school," their father told them even though they always came home right after school, except on Tuesdays and Thursdays when they went to Mrs. Valenti's. Before the riots started in April and classes were cancelled, those were the days that their father went to the city to teach his classes.

Mrs. Valenti was an old Italian woman who lived near the school. They didn't really like going to her house, but they didn't hate it either. It was not a stimulating environment because Mrs. Valenti just sat in front of the tv and knitted, but they were used to entertaining themselves. They called Tuesdays and Thursdays their quiet days because Mrs. Valenti was afraid to let them walk to the park or go downtown by themselves, and she certainly had no desire to go with them, so they usually just read or drew and sometimes they made up little plays, which they acted out for Mrs. Valenti, who tried her best to show interest in the performance while keeping track of her television show at the same time. Mrs. Valenti called them *my sweet little girls*, and they always had some kind of spaghetti for dinner. Still, even though they both loved spaghetti, if they were given a choice, they would always choose to come home rather than go to Mrs. Valenti's house.

Since this past winter, however, which was when their father had met Mrs. Tuttle, the girls had been spending more than just Tuesdays and Thursdays with Mrs. Valenti, though their father made it a policy not to leave them in her charge more than three days a week. Mrs. Tuttle was a secretary at the offices of the publishing house that was putting out a college textbook on modern European history, for which their father was writing the chapters pertaining to Russia and the Soviet Union.

Mrs. Tuttle brought them books from her publishing company. She gave them wonderful hardcover volumes from a series called the Dual Classics. Each volume in the series contained two classic unabridged novels. If, for example, one opened the book from one side, it was *Call of the Wild*, and if one turned it over and opened it from the other side, it was *Robinson Crusoe*. Mrs. Tuttle also brought them the books *Coming of Age in Mississippi*, *Lilies of the Field*, and *Black Like Me*. Juliet and Simone actually liked these books better than those in the Dual Classics because they dealt with what they called *real life*, not with such far-flung topics as desert islands and freezing to death in the wilds of Alaska. Still, there was something about the "duality" that they were especially intrigued by, and for this reason the Dual Classics were all prominently displayed in a neat row on the top, and most important, shelf of their bookcase. The dramas they acted out, however, were inspired not by the Dual Classics but by *Coming of Age in Mississippi*, which was by far their favorite. The skits were about the adventures of two poor black sisters who were the smartest children in their class even though they didn't own a pair of shoes.

Mrs. Tuttle did not visit very often because she and their father usually had their own plans, which involved dinner out and excursions to the city, but sometimes she came for dinner or for tea on Sunday afternoon. On one such Sunday, Juliet had convinced Simone to perform the latest chapter in the adventures of the two poor black sisters for Mrs. Tuttle and their father. They spent a lot of time preparing, much more time than they ever spent preparing for Mrs. Valenti. They put on dresses and knee socks and the straw hats that they had gotten at Jones Beach. Then they went through the skit twice, making sure their southern accents didn't slip into Russian accents, which was often what happened whenever they attempted a new type of accent. They could not, however, imitate their father's accent because they could not hear it, though he himself had explained to them that it most certainly existed. He described it as *hard to place.* This he attributed to the fact that he had spent his childhood and youth fleeing with his parents first from Russia, then from Germany, and then from France. As a result, he did not have a mother tongue, and he often reminded Juliet and Simone that they were lucky to have a mother tongue, though they were not sure that having one was superior to knowing how to speak four languages fluently, as their father did.

They came down the stairs slowly and sheepishly entered the living room where their father and Mrs. Tuttle were waiting. "Don't you look nice," Mrs. Tuttle said, and they blushed.

The drama they had selected for Mrs. Tuttle's entertainment was about what happened to the sisters in school one day when one of them, Juliet, told her white teacher that when she grew up she wanted to be a paleontologist like Dr. Richard Leakey. Simone played the roles of the white teacher and the older sister.

"Where did you hear about Dr. Richard Leakey?" the teacher asked sternly.

"In *National Geographic,*" Juliet said proudly. Then the teacher accused poor Juliet of stealing the *National Geographic*, and Juliet defiantly insisted that she had bought it with her own money, saved up for weeks and weeks, but the teacher wouldn't believe her and beat her over the head with a yardstick until she fell to the ground covered in blood and an ambulance had to be called. Simone, the teacher, kept repeating over and over again, "Take her to the Negro hospital! Take her to the Negro hospital!" During the bludgeoning scene, Simone had deftly squeezed tomato paste, which she had put in a carefully constructed tube of tinfoil, over Juliet's face as she was hitting her with the ruler, so Juliet's face and dress were splotched with tomato paste. The drama ended with Simone pulling the unconscious Juliet along the floor to the ambulance that waited outside. Then they returned for a shy bow and a curtsy too, for good measure. They looked up and smiled. Their father produced five cursory claps but neither he nor Mrs. Tuttle smiled.

Juliet and Simone did not quite understand why their skit was unsuccessful, though they were sufficiently embarrassed not to ask their father to explain it to them, nor did he offer any explanations. They knew it had something to do with the fact that they were white and Mrs. Tuttle was black, but that was as far as they got. The next time they saw Mrs. Tuttle, she gave them both kisses as usual and three biographies—of Eleanor Roosevelt, Madame Curie, and Betsy Ross—all of which they found tiresome, though Eleanor Roosevelt's clothing reminded them of Mrs. Tuttle's, and after that they always thought of Mrs. Tuttle when they saw a photograph of Eleanor Roosevelt in one of their textbooks or on a stamp.

Juliet and Simone ran up the hill so they would be home right after school as their father had requested. They were not able to put into words what it was they had expected to find at home, but Jakobson was still there, sitting in the backyard with ashes on his clothes, smoking his cigar. He seemed calmer than yesterday, too calm almost, as if he were just about to nod off. On the table were three tall glasses of what looked like the special yoghurt, rice, banana, almond, honey, orange, and ginger shakes that their father made for them when they were sick. They were surprised to find Mrs. Tuttle there too, wearing a lilac-colored spring suit that somehow made her look even more serious than the gray and brown ones did. "Why's she here?" Juliet whispered to Simone, for Mrs. Tuttle never just stopped by.

"Maybe Dad needed some help," Simone whispered back.

"Help with what?"

"With Jakobson," Simone said.

"What are you two whispering about?" Jakobson said. "If you

have something to say, say it. All these secrets. I can't stand all these secrets."

"Sorry," Simone said. "We didn't mean to be rude." She turned to Mrs. Tuttle and demonstrated her good manners, using her father's favorite greeting. "Hello, Mrs. Tuttle. To what do we owe the pleasure of your company?"

Mrs. Tuttle smiled. "Hello, Simone," she said.

Simone pinched Juliet lightly on the back, and Juliet went over to greet Mrs. Tuttle. "So how are you girls doing?" she asked.

"Fine," they said in unison.

Then everyone was silent. Jakobson was staring up at the sky, looking right up into the sun without blinking.

"Mrs. Tuttle's son is in the war," Juliet said. Juliet did not like silences.

Jakobson flinched as if someone had crept up from behind and put a hand on his shoulder. He turned toward Mrs. Tuttle and stared at her as he had been staring at the sun.

"Assassin," Jakobson said softly, whispering almost. Then he turned his back to Mrs. Tuttle.

Mrs. Tuttle's lips quivered, but she did not respond. She closed her eyes, and their father put his hand on her hand. "Are you okay?" their father asked her.

"I'll be fine, Isaac," she said, patting their father's hand. "He really should try some of that shake," she said.

Their father picked up the glass that was sitting on the table next to Jakobson. "Jakobson, why don't you have some of this shake? You can't starve yourself to death," their father said, trying to put a glass into Jakobson's hand.

"I have no desire to eat," Jakobson said, pushing the glass away.

"I am not asking you to eat," their father said. "I am asking you to drink." He pointed to the milkshake and Jakobson looked at it sadly.

"This is no time to split hairs, Isaac," Jakobson said, picking up the glass and holding it up to the light. He removed his glasses and scrutinized the drink. "No, I don't think I'm up for it," he said, setting the glass down again.

"Suit yourself," their father said.

Mrs. Tuttle took a sip from her own shake, lifting the glass to her lips, drinking, setting it down on the table again slowly as if she were demonstrating for Jakobson how to do it, but he did not notice. He was preoccupied with a bee that was buzzing around his head. He kept swatting it away, but back it would come, circling and making dives toward his beard. The more he swatted at it, the more intent upon settling down on Jakobson's beard the bee seemed to be. "Ignore it, Jakobson," their father said, but Jakobson said, "You wouldn't be able to ignore it either if it were buzzing madly around your head."

All of a sudden, the bee lost interest in Jakobson and dove at Mrs. Tuttle, landing on her hand and stinging her. Mrs. Tuttle did not jump up or cry out. She simply held her hand up in the air as if she were about to wave and had changed her mind. "I think it stung me," she said.

Mrs. Tuttle's hand was blowing up. It was easily twice the size of her unstung hand and her face was getting puffy—her eyes seemed lost and small in her head. Mrs. Tuttle said, "Isaac, I don't think I can breathe," and their father said they had to get to the hospital as fast as possible.

"Keep an eye on Jakobson," he whispered as they followed him and Mrs. Tuttle to the garage, "and don't let him smoke in the house."

"Bee stings can be very dangerous, very, very dangerous," Jakobson said when Juliet and Simone returned to the garden. "If your throat swells up enough, then you can't breathe and then, well, it is very dangerous."

Simone and Juliet sat stiffly in the chairs opposite his. They did not want to leave him alone because their father had told them to keep an eye on him, and they were sure that if he were left to his own devices, the first thing he would do would be to go inside the house and light up a cigar.

"Is Mrs. Tuttle going to die?" Juliet asked.

Jakobson laughed. It was the first time he laughed since he had arrived the day before. "Do you like Mrs. Tuttle?" he asked.

"Of course I like her," Juliet said.

"Why of course? Is there a rule that says you have to like Mrs. Tuttle?" Jakobson asked, leaning forward in his chair so Juliet could smell his cigar breath as he spoke.

"There's no rule. I just like her. Don't you like her?" Juliet asked, leaning forward in her chair the way Jakobson had done.

"I don't really know her. She seems a little stiff, don't you think?"

"Stiff?" Juliet asked. "She's tall. Is that what you mean?"

"She's just serious," Simone said. "What's wrong with being serious?"

"Nothing, there's nothing wrong with being serious. Life is a serious affair."

"Do you think she'll be okay?" Simone asked. She hadn't realized until that very moment that she was shaking.

"I am not a soothsayer," Jakobson said. "If I were a soothsayer, all this would never have happened." Jakobson punched himself in the head. He punched himself again, this time with the other fist, and then again and again and again. "Idiot, idiot, idiot," he repeated over and over.

Juliet and Simone did not know how to stop him, so they remained in their chairs, watching, keeping an eye on him as their father had told them to do. Simone tried not to look him directly in the eye. She focused instead on the branch of the apple tree slightly above his head. Juliet was humming softly to herself the way she did when she was concentrating on her homework or her dinner.

Then they heard the phone ringing. "You stay here," Simone said to Juliet, and she ran inside.

Several minutes later, Simone ran back outside and announced, "Mrs. Tuttle is fine. My father's taking her home and then he'll be back. Mrs. Tuttle is going to be just fine!" She felt her voice rise at the end of her proclamation. Juliet pointed at Jakobson, who was still punching himself—his glasses had fallen to the ground.

"He'll be home soon," Simone said taking her sister's hand. "Why don't you go inside? I can watch Jakobson." So Juliet went inside. She went up to her room and got under the covers with all her clothes on, including her shoes. Under the covers she could smell the rubber of her sneakers and the detergent from the clean sheets mixing together. She lay very quietly, inhaling the smell from her sneakers and the sheets, until she heard her father's key in the door, at which point she jumped out of her bed and ran down the stairs three steps at a time to greet him.

"Jakobson is punching himself," Juliet told her father calmly, though her heart was racing and her palms were sweating. "Simone's out there with him. We didn't leave him alone for a second."

"Well, let's see what we can do for the poor fellow." Isaac took his daughter's hand and they walked outside, but no words of encouragement or reason could make Jakobson stop punching himself and muttering, "Idiot, idiot, idiot."

"Why didn't Mrs. Tuttle come back for dinner?" Juliet asked as all three of them sat there keeping an eye on Jakobson.

"She had to rest," Isaac said.

"She could rest here," Juliet said.

"Not with Jakobson here," their father explained. "It's too much commotion."

"I guess you're right," Juliet said.

"Now what are we going to do with Jakobson?"

"Maybe he'll sleep if we bring him upstairs again," Simone suggested.

Their father tried coaxing Jakobson out of his chair, but this only made him punch himself more furiously, so they all went inside to prepare dinner, hoping that Jakobson would be less inclined to continue his latest drama if he had no audience. Every ten minutes or so their father sent Simone out to check on him and the report was always the same: Jakobson was still punching himself. When it got dark, after they had finished dinner and washed the dishes, he was still punching himself. Just before they went to sleep, Simone and Juliet looked out their window and down at Jakobson—a dark shadow and a spark of light from his cigar. That was Jakobson. They could not see that he was punching himself, but they knew that he was—with one hand while the other held the cigar.

In the morning Jakobson was gone. Their father had called an ambulance in the middle of the night and it had come and taken him away. Simone and Juliet had not heard anything.

"Did the ambulance have its siren on?" Juliet asked.

"No, it was not that kind of emergency," their father told them.

"I didn't think so. We would have heard it if the siren was on," Juliet said, still wondering how they could have slept through it all, for surely Jakobson had put up a fight.

A few days after they took Jakobson away, their father called Simone and Juliet into the living room. "I have sad news," he said once they were all seated. "We will not be seeing Mrs. Tuttle anymore."

For a moment they both thought that Mrs. Tuttle had died and their hearts started beating fast like the time they hit a patch of ice, and their father lost control of the car for a split second, regaining it just in time to avoid crashing into a truck. "But you told us that she was okay, that they caught it in time," Juliet said.

Their father laughed, and then they knew that Mrs. Tuttle was not dead. "Mrs. Tuttle is very much alive," he said. "We have just decided that it would be best not to continue our friendship."

"Because of what Jakobson said about her son?" Simone asked.

"That was only the straw that broke the camel's back," their father said, and Simone pictured Mrs. Tuttle bent over so that her back was nearly parallel to the ground, straining in the hot sun under an enormous bundle of straw. She imagined Mrs. Tuttle's son, too. He is waiting in the hot jungle, his gun poised. He hears a sound in the underbrush. He turns, shoots. A bird flies out of the thick underbrush and to the safety of a tree. Then silence.

"Do you think he'll be all right?" Simone said.

"Jakobson?"

"No, Mrs. Tuttle's son," Simone said.

"I don't know," her father said, shaking his head. "I don't know."

the boys of el tambor

Dear Amy,

I don't know exactly how I got here or why I'm here. I know I left during the windy season. I had been thinking about leaving for a long time, but the day I actually left, the wind was gusting at fifty miles an hour. There were huge branches lying in almost every yard. That is the last impression I have of Albuquerque—the broken branches and the wind trying to push my car off the road as I headed south on I-25 and the dust blowing around so that I could hardly see. I thought for a moment that it was all an omen, but then I remembered that I don't believe in omens. Sometimes I wish I did. It would simplify things, help me make decisions.

I don't know how many days it took me to get here or why I decided that this was the place to stop. I could have kept going; I had not run out of money. But there was something I liked about Coatzacoalcos, though there's nothing beautiful about it. Nothing. It's dirty and poor and smells like a combination of sea air and rotten fruit. The landscape is dull, flat. There is just one small hill. The town's main attraction, if you could call it that, is the promenade. Everyone tells me that it's dangerous to walk along the promenade alone, but I always do, and nothing has happened to me yet.

As far as I know, I am the only foreigner who has stayed here in a long time. There's something comforting about knowing that I won't come in contact with another American. Not that I have anything against Americans—after all, I am one—but I am not in the mood to answer questions. Americans would want to dig. They would be sure of my unhappiness, but the truth is that here I feel neither unhappy nor happy. I know you would say that this is not possible, that if one is not happy one must be unhappy, but for you everything is always black or white. In any case, the townspeople of Coatzacoalcos don't ask too many questions. They're satisfied with knowing where I am from, how old I am, and that I am not married. This suits me well. It is, I suppose, what I was looking for and why I stay.

I have been here for about three months. Who knows, I might stay here forever. I might just write to Ginny and Beth and tell them to clean out my apartment, sell what they can, keep what they want, give the rest away. I don't need any of it. I wrote to Tony at the bar to let him know I wasn't coming back to work. I probably should have called him instead of disappearing like that, leaving him shorthanded. I actually miss the bar more than anything else. It became my home after you left. I actually felt wanted there, needed, stupid as that may sound. People told me things they couldn't tell anyone else. They knew their misery was safe with me.

When I left, I thought I might get back to painting once I was far away, once I didn't have to think about you twenty-four hours a day. But I am not painting. In fact, I have decided not to think about my paintings anymore. What's the point? They're too disturbing and no one likes it anyway, except for you, but what does that matter now? I think the last thing you ever said to me, when you were so bluntly, so honestly, explaining to me why you no longer loved me, was "You don't even goddamn paint anymore." As if anyone cared. All anyone wants to see are pastel colors and soft mountains and big skies. No one wants to see what I see—shadows on black or dark fires. I couldn't even sell my paintings in New York, where they're supposed to like dark. I got sick of getting my portfolio back with a scribbled note: "Very moving and disturbing work, but it's not quite right for our gallery." You used to say to just fuck them and keep on painting, but you don't know how hard that gets. At least your stories get published, even if it's only in stiff literary magazines and obscure feminist publications that practically no one reads.

Here life is simple. No one asks me when I'm going to start painting again because no one knows I paint. No one asks me about you because no one knows you exist. Sometimes I even pretend that I don't know Spanish, and no one suspects that I actually grew up speaking it because, of course, I don't look like I speak Spanish. I haven't even written to my parents to tell them where I am. I guess one of these days when my mother is feeling bad about us not being close, or my father stops spending all his free time trying to make sure my mother doesn't have a breakdown, they'll try to call me. Maybe they already have, but I doubt it. One of these days I'll send them a postcard just so they don't get freaked out when they call and the phone is disconnected.

You probably want to know how I'm making a living down here. You're always interested in practical matters. I know you'll think my job is demeaning, but I like the work. I like mopping the cool tile floors. I like shaking out the rugs. I like hanging heavy white linen sheets on the line to dry. And I like Marta and Rafael. I suppose you could call them my bosses, but I feel comfortable with them, especially with Marta. In the evenings, we sit out on their balcony and drink tequila. Just because they're rich doesn't mean they're jerks. That's one thing that you could never understand about people. I know. We've been through this before. I don't know what it's like not to have money, but it's not like you grew up in the projects in the South Bronx and I am the daughter of millionaires. After all, you lived in a house on Long Island and went to school and your father had a job, but you always said that wasn't the point, and I guess, on some level, it wasn't.

I look forward to my work here. Actually, there really isn't enough for me to do in the house to warrant employing me full-time, but Marta always scrounges up something to keep me busy. Today she had me polish the silverware. There were twelve boxes of it, all heirlooms from her side of the family. I think she likes having me around because Rafael is out all day recording or he's on the road. He's a musician. The whole living room is filled with photographs of Rafael and his salsa band. Some of them are posed studio shots and some are just pictures taken while they were playing or hanging out—trumpets shining, rounded drums, white pants, smiles, legs, hips, guitars, tropical shirts, open mouths. There are a lot of open mouths, a lot of legs. Sometimes she is in the pictures also, looking off into the distance as if she were waiting for a ship to appear on the horizon.

I have told Marta very little about myself. She knows I'm from New York, that most recently I lived in Albuquerque. Like I said, she doesn't ask questions. Sometimes I have this incredible desire to tell her everything, about you, about Gilbert, and I try to picture myself telling her. We're out on the balcony. There's a cool breeze, and she is smoking, looking out at the Gulf. There are three tankers in view, but they're still far out. We prepare to drink a shot of tequila. We drink, set our glasses back down on the table. And that is as far as I get. If you start telling someone something important, you begin to expect them to understand you, and that is dangerous. I guess the reason that Marta and I are comfortable together is precisely because we don't talk much. We listen to music; we watch the Gulf. But most of the time I'm busy with my tasks—polishing the silver, oiling the teak furniture, folding the laundry.

I like the physical work. At night, when I finally go to sleep, I'm actually tired. I have not felt that way in a long time, not since I was a child, when I would play tennis all day long in the blazing sun or spend hours and hours in the town pool until my lips turned purple and then even longer than that. You used to try to get me to go on hikes, but I would just wait somewhere on a rock and sketch. I should have gone hiking with you. I don't know why I didn't, why I was so opposed to physical activity. I never used to be like that. I have stopped drawing too.

At first, when I stopped painting, it was difficult to find other things to occupy my time. I would try to read, but after ten minutes, I grew restless. I couldn't even concentrate at the movies. Of course you know all this. But you must remember too when I used to lock myself in the studio and paint for three days straight, stopping only when you called me to the table for dinner. But you didn't like it when I was too involved in my painting either. It wasn't healthy, you said, to be so obsessed, as if my art were some kind of illness. I never said that about your writing.

When I told you I was never going to paint again, you thought I was exaggerating in my usual melodramatic fashion. "Why do you always have to go to extremes? Just because I said that it would be good for you to get out more, to diversify," you said, like it was some kind of business decision.

"You don't understand; this is it. This is the end," I tried to explain, but you just laughed.

"You can't plan your future anyway because you don't know what's going to happen. No one ever knows what's going to happen," you said.

You always liked saying things like that, like, You never know, one day you might be madly in love with one person, and then the next day, you might meet someone new in a café, and by evening, your whole life will have changed. I guess that's just another way we're different. We have different definitions of "madly in love."

I'm going out now. I can't stand lying on the bed in this dumpy hotel a moment longer. I'm going to El Tambor. I'll tell you about it tomorrow.

I have been rereading what I have written, and I don't exactly know why I bothered to tell you all this in such detail, but I will continue because I have no one else who will have the patience to slog through it all. I was going to tell you about El Tambor. It's a sleazy bar where all the drag queens hang out. Of course, you hated the bars. You always got angry about the music and would start complaining about how everyone was acting like a stereotype—either that, or they were depressing alcoholics. "What do we have in common with these people?" you asked, and I told you that it made me feel comfortable to be around other gay people even if we didn't have much to say to each other, and you said that was stupid and depressing, that you didn't want to be just some stereotype, and that would be the end of the discussion because I didn't want to have to think about what it was you were really saying whether you knew it or not. Anyway, El Tambor makes me feel at home. The minute I walked in, the bartender smiled that smile that says, *You are one of us.*

But I'm not the only one who finds it comfortable. Marta likes it, too, and she's not a lesbian. And the prostitutes that work the regular bars along the port come here when they need a break—to put aside the act, have a drink for the sake of having a drink. Recently, one of the prostitutes tried to sell me one of her six children, whom she supports without anyone's help. "American women like you want children," she informed me, and I wasn't angry at her for making a generalization about Americans or lesbians. I wasn't even angry at her for trying to get rid of one of her children. "My youngest daughter is very sweet and very smart, but not tough. I worry about her all the time. When she gets older, her life will be very difficult," she said, and then added in English, in order to make her offer perfectly clear, "very cheap, very cheap."

I thanked her politely as if she were selling handicrafts rather than a child, and she shook her head and walked away.

The next morning while I was oiling Marta's banister, I kept thinking about what it would be like to have a little girl, how I would teach her English and how to ride a bicycle and take her to visit my parents in New York, but you were the one who wanted children. You were the one who was always saying that I should adopt because I'm so good with children, but I understand now that I'm good with them because I don't want to have them. Still, I would have adopted a child with you if that's what you wanted, but you didn't want to adopt. You wanted your own child. I wouldn't even be surprised if you were pregnant right now, wishing that I were around so you could call me up and tell me the good news. You'll probably want me to be the godmother, but I don't think that's a good idea since I don't believe in God even though you always tried to convince me that I really did.

But I was telling you about El Tambor. It's completely pink. There's not one wall, one chair or tabletop that is not bright pink. Even the napkins are pink, and the toilet paper, when there is toilet paper. The only thing about El Tambor I don't like is Alberto, the owner. He's about fifty and always wears a white linen suit and a white shirt, and his stomach hangs way out over his snakeskin belt. He doesn't do much of anything. He doesn't talk or get in anyone's way. He just sits sullenly in a corner drinking Cuba libres and smoking. I've seen him drink up to fifteen in a night, but he never seems drunk. I don't think I've ever seen him smile, and he's even sullen when he's with his boy. The boy sits quietly next to him, holding his hand, and Alberto doesn't pay the boy any attention unless he gets up and starts talking to someone else. Then Alberto gives him an angry look and the boy returns to Alberto's table. Since I've been coming to El Tambor, he's been through six boys. And they *are* boys—thirteen, fourteen, sixteen at the most. They're all thin and dark with big, Indian eyes. Right now he is with Jesús. Even though I like to pride myself on being open-minded, the idea of Alberto touching Jesús makes me sick. I once told Marta this and she laughed. "You Americans are such Puritans," she said. But it's not that. Maybe it's because of Gilbert.

Do you know that there were times when I wanted to smash Gilbert's face in with my boots, dig my heel into his puffy, hairy chest, smash his nose into his skull? But, of course, I'm too civilized for that kind of behavior, too polite, too cool. Not even a caustic phrase crossed my lips when I was in his presence. And then I would go home and fling my books around the apartment and slam the doors and smash the glass on the paintings, my paintings, and when you returned from a weekend in Taos with Gilbert, you didn't even acknowledge the signs of my wrath, didn't even ask what happened to the glass or why the books were all out of order. You kissed me and I could feel that your lips were rougher than they had been before Gilbert, and I would recoil and storm out of the house, and when I returned, you would try to comfort me, tell me to be patient, that you needed us both, that you were working things out, and I would hold on to you as if we were both drowning, and all I could see were his big hands on your breasts and his hard, hairy face resting on your stomach, and I couldn't stand to be near you any longer, so I locked myself in my studio for hours, all night long. But I did not paint.

At first, I think I stopped painting out of spite, because I knew it was the thing you most admired about me. But I guess it wasn't enough. Still, an academic? You used to despise college professors. You had your whole ivory-tower harangue. But I suppose Gilbert is different because he spent a year volunteering in Guatemala and wears colorful, hand-woven shirts, not ties and jackets. But after a while I could not have painted even if I had wanted to, and it's not because of Gilbert or, as you implied, because I'm too conventional, because a real artist, a true Bohemian, would be proud of the fact that her girlfriend had so much love to go around. But I don't want to dwell on things. I came here to get away from that. I'll go to El Tambor, have a few drinks, dance. I'll joke with the drag queens, listen to them tell me for the fiftieth time that they will be leaving Coatzacoalcos soon, leaving for Amsterdam where a girl can be a girl and walk down the street in heels without having rocks hurled at her. I suppose my life could be worse. I could have been born a queen in Mexico.

I haven't told you about all the aspects of my relationship with Marta and Rafael, but you wouldn't have the whole picture if I didn't. I suppose I could stop everything, but I don't really want to. It is a sort of strange exercise for me, an exercise in what, I'm not quite sure yet, but I suppose I will figure it out at some point. All I know is that I find our sessions together pleasant. It's like doing some odd form of meditation, not that I've ever tried meditation, but I suppose it must be something like that when I'm with them. There's no thinking involved, no emotion, just a rhythm, a movement. I get so tired of having to live with my mind and my thoughts and with this anger that doesn't seem to go away. Sometimes it subsides, but it is always there, waiting for me when I'm most vulnerable, when I'm falling asleep at night or walking alone near the water in the hot sun. Then I will envision you and Gilbert holding hands or worse, and my whole body will begin throbbing with rage, and the only thing that can help is tequila and Marta and Rafael.

How did it start? I was trying to remember. I don't think there were any words spoken. We were all drinking out on the balcony. It was already dark but still very hot. One of Rafael's records was playing in the background, softly so you could only hear the music if you listened for it carefully. Then Rafael got up and went inside without excusing himself. Marta and I stayed on the balcony for a while longer, I couldn't say how long, and then she got up too, and I followed her. Maybe she said something, like "come with me," but I don't think so. I followed her upstairs and into their bedroom. Rafael was lying naked on the bed. He was beautiful—his brown body on the white sheets that I had ironed. And so we started. Sometimes when we are finished, I stay for dinner and sometimes I don't. Sometimes I just go to El Tambor by myself afterward. Sometimes Marta and I go together. Rafael rarely joins us there. I don't know whether this is because El Tambor makes him uncomfortable or because he goes someplace else to be with his musician friends. As I said, we don't talk much. I don't know whether they planned it or whether it just happened, but it doesn't really matter either way.

In the beginning, I thought that I was doing it because it was the only way I had of understanding you. But I understand now that it has very little to do with you because you are in love with Gilbert, or so you claim, and I am not in love with either of them. I am happy to leave them when I do, glad to be able to go back to my hotel room even though it's so unbearably hot and you can hear the din from the cantinas all night long. I don't think I could spend a night in their house. It's so big, so clean, so empty.

I know it's clean because I clean it every day. If you can believe it, I have become fastidious and neat. If we got back together, which I know we will not, which I would not want to do under any circumstances, we wouldn't fight about whose turn it was to clean the bathroom anymore. I would just do it.

You probably think that what I'm doing is disgusting, not the sex itself but the wallowing. But so what if I'm wallowing? Maybe that's what I need. And sometimes I even feel happy, or if not happy, energetic. Maybe someday I will be able to enjoy the simple things like watching a child play or ice cream, and then you will be able to say, "I told you so. I told you that it's the simple things that make us happy."

Or maybe what I'm doing is not wallowing at all. Maybe I'm just trying to feel alive, and they are both gentle and smell good and the sound of their breathing soothes me. As a matter of fact, I can hear their voices coming from the driveway now. They have spent the day in the country; they went to some village, where there was a festival, a religious one, of course. They didn't ask me to go with them, and I didn't feel left out. They're laughing. I suppose they are happy. Soon, we will be sitting outside on the balcony, drinking, watching the water, smiling at each other. And then we will go up to their room. I could describe to you exactly what happens when we are together, but you are probably not interested, and if you were, you would never admit it. Or you would say that you are surprised by my behavior, that it is so unlike me. But I don't find it unlike me at all.

Tonight is Alberto's birthday, and he's throwing a huge party at El Tambor. Everyone is invited, and all drinks and food are on the house. Apparently it's the event of the year. They're roasting thirty pigs right now. I can smell them from my room. The smell of roasting pig combined with the Gulf's particular watery smell that is like rain on concrete mixed with garbage and fish and fruit is turning my stomach. I have gotten used to the smell of the Gulf, but the added porky odor is too much. If you were here, you would refuse to go. You would say that you didn't want to take part in this paternalistic travesty—the rich landlord throwing scraps to the peasants. But that is the way the world works. I'm sure there will be plenty of boys there too—perfect, smooth boys with large eyes and small asses and tight bellies. I wonder how many of them Alberto will take home with him tonight.

The women at those dreadful women's poetry readings you

dragged me to would be horrified by tonight's events. Didn't one of them change her name to Salad Average? What the hell was that supposed to mean? But I'd rather go to El Tambor than sit on uncomfortable folding chairs trying not to laugh. I never understood how you could stand listening to all that bad writing about amazons and incest survivors. That one about the brown-skinned woman nearly sent me over the edge. How did it go? "My brown-skinned woman. How I love my brown-skinned woman, my brown-skinned woman, I love her, my brown-skinned woman." Do you still believe that the quality of the art is not what matters, that what is important is for women to express themselves? You always said that good art would come later, once we were free. Well, I'm free now, so maybe I will start painting again any day now. Maybe my art will reach new heights. Does Gilbert go with you to the readings now? Does he feel proud to be there, to be a part of this wonderful expression of liberation and community?

In some ways, it would be amusing if you came for a visit. You could even bring Gilbert. He would like it—the poverty, the exploitation. He could write an article. I could take you to the jungle to see the Indians. But then I would have to tell Marta and Rafael who you were, and that would spoil everything, though you would say that it would make me feel better to talk about how I'm feeling. But I have told you everything, and I don't feel better. I just feel empty, like you've taken everything from me once again even though it was my idea to write you this letter.

I don't really know where to begin about last night. I'm still at that piecing-together stage and am trying to uncover what was veiled in the mist of alcohol. I know—I shouldn't drink so much, it worries you, but you're not here, and anyway you know I go through phases. I'm like my mother that way, I guess. Sometimes I just have to drink more than I should. It helps me think. Actually, I do remember. It's just a question of digging it out of the rubble of the evening. I like that about hangovers. I like waking up with dirty fingernails and my hair reeking of smoke and my legs aching. It gives me the right to take it easy, to linger under the shower, eat a good breakfast, take a long nap, go over everything in my head. And I don't have to do anything today. Marta and Rafael have gone to Veracruz for a week. They gave me the keys to their house in case I want to relax in a more comfortable environment, but I think I'll stay here despite the heat and the smell of mold. It will be a challenge to see whether I can hold out, whether I can keep myself from caving in to luxury.

But I was going to tell you about the party. The revelers spilled out into the streets along the waterfront and onto the piers, and we ate all thirty pigs. In the morning the streets were covered with bones. Even I had some, not too much because you know I don't like to eat pork, but it wouldn't have been polite to refuse. Alberto carved up the pigs himself, and his boys handed out chunks of meat as people walked by the spit. Everyone was there—even the priests, who were just as drunk as everyone else.

Despite the festivities, Alberto was more morose than usual. When there was no pork left, he went back inside. Shortly after that, I started feeling tired, so I went inside the bar and sat down with the queens. Marta and Rafael were dancing anyway, so there wasn't much point in just watching them. You probably think that I should have felt bad about being left out, but I didn't. I was happy to sit with the queens. They just chattered away, and I smiled at their self-deprecating jokes, but I didn't have to say anything. No one was paying any attention to Alberto, not even the boys, and I remember feeling bad for him, thinking how lonely he must be sitting there all alone on his birthday, but then my eyes locked on his stomach straining the buttons of his shirt, and I couldn't help imagining him with Jesús. I saw him lying on his back in an overly soft bed, his body sinking deep down into the mattress, his huge stomach sticking up into the air, wobbling a little back and forth like Jell-O, while Jesús sucked on his wrinkled dick. I could see the sweat running down the slopes of his paunch, soaking the sheets, and then I saw Alberto on top of Jesús, fucking him hard in the ass, his belly flopping on the boy's smooth back, and then the boy's face turned into your face and I wanted to scream but I didn't, and then I noticed that Alberto was staring at me, looking right into my eyes, just smoking and staring. "Come here," he called to me. "Come sit down." It was not an invitation but a command, and I obeyed.

"You are like me," he said. "I have been throwing this party every year on my birthday for eight years. It was eight years ago on this day that the only person I ever loved left me. He ran away, went back to his village in the jungle. He was just a boy. He missed his mother. I told him that I would bring his mother here—I would buy her a house, and he could see her whenever he wanted—but he left anyway. I could have sent someone to get him, to bring him back, but instead I hold these parties in his honor." There were tears in Alberto's eyes, real tears.

"Yes, I am like you," I said, and he smiled and called for a bottle of tequila, and we drank together and talked about insignificant things until the sun came in through the pink curtains and the queens went home without saying good-bye. Then I helped Alberto close up and we walked through the town, stepping over drunken bodies and pig bones, and when we came to my hotel, we parted, and I watched him walk slowly, yet in a perfectly straight line, back up the hill toward his house.

I think it is time for me to move on. Perhaps I will go back to Albuquerque or New York. Perhaps I will continue south. Maybe I should use this opportunity to travel a little, see the world. I could go to Bolivia, go to the town where my mother and my grandparents spent the war years. Maybe there are some people who still remember them. Of course I will not send you this letter. What would be the point? I don't want to upset you, and you would just get upset. Instead I will send you a postcard—a picture of the market with lots of colorful fruits and fabrics. I will write, "Am in Mexico enjoying a different surrounding. Please don't worry."

Love always,
Ester

after the war

Karl would have stayed there in Bolivia, where nothing ever changed, even though they had a coup every six months. The papers did not even bother to print that kind of news on the front page, so one only found out about a change in government if one read the pages with the obituaries. He could have worked his way into that hot, wet world, and perhaps one day, the people of Rurrenabaque would have forgotten that he had not always lived there. He could have gotten into the habit of getting up late and spending the long hot nights arguing until his throat hurt about whether taking up arms and getting rid of the generals once and for all was worth it.

But Margot, his wife, was always complaining about the singing in the streets that disturbed her insomniac nights. She couldn't stand the little statues of the Virgin that stared down at her from the wall when she tried to have an afternoon coffee in the only halfway-clean restaurant in town. She said that Spanish was a language for short, fat old women chattering away in the marketplace. She had always hated old women. Perhaps most of all, she hated Bolivia for its women who were old at forty and dead at fifty, dressed in simple black (for their husbands had died earlier), lying with their hands folded across their breasts, holding a simple crucifix.

Karl had been pulled into Bolivia from the moment they arrived. He had devoured a Spanish grammar on the boat, and that, in combination with his medical-school Latin, made it possible for him to communicate immediately. In the beginning, he spent the afternoons reading the newspaper, underlining all the words he didn't know and then compiling them into lists, which he would memorize and repeat to himself almost like a prayer as he made his rounds, on foot in town and by boat to the outlying villages along the river.

He had even suggested once that they stay in Bolivia after the war was over. They could send their daughter Sonya to the International School in La Paz. But Margot said that it would have been better to remain in Vienna and die with the others in the gas chambers than to stay there in all that dampness and noise.

Even after two years, Karl has not been able to settle into life in New York, though there are things he likes about their new home—the opera, Carnegie Hall. But there is so little time for music here, so little time to think, except for now at the end of the workday, when he can sit for a little while in his office with the lights off and look out the window at the gray and hard Bronx. He has finished with his last patient, and the nurse has just gone home, left him as she does every evening with the same words: "Good night, Dr. Epstein. We'll see you tomorrow, same time, same place."

No, he cannot get used to New York. So what that there is a Jewish deli where they can get fresh rye bread and lox and potato salad? So what that they can play bridge with their neighbors? So what that there is a nice temple with nice people right down the street? They never go anyway. After what they went through, with the Nazis practically at their door, and his mother, his old and nearly blind mother, and both Margot's sisters, and the countless cousins and aunts and uncles all dead, they have no desire to go to temple. They don't even light the candles on Friday nights anymore, though they did in Bolivia. Somehow it had made more sense there.

And how many patients has he seen today? He cannot even remember their names or their ailments. All he knows is that he has seen too many because he is so tired now that he could fall asleep right here in the chair at his desk in his dark, quiet office. He has no energy left to walk the fifteen blocks home. And this has been a particularly cold winter. The Hudson River is completely frozen over. Last Sunday he and Sonya walked on it. They walked from New York to New Jersey and back to New York on the Hudson River, and when they got home, they drank hot chocolate and ate éclairs that they bought from Fleischman's Bakery.

No, he really doesn't want to go home tonight. He would much rather sit here and doze. Later he could run downstairs and get a sandwich for dinner; he could smoke a cigar. Margot doesn't let him smoke his cigars in the house. He wonders how she is feeling tonight. Has she had the energy to cook dinner? Has she made a nice heavy stew with plenty of potatoes and carrots? Is there fresh bread? Is she sitting in the living room on the couch they just bought from Bamberger's, waiting for him to come home? Or is she lying on the unmade bed in her bathrobe with all the shades drawn, and has she been that way all afternoon so that when he gets home, he will have to sit with her, just sit there in the dark? And then he will heat up some soup and try to get her to eat, to sit up, to listen to the radio.

He must go home. He has to think of Sonya. She has been doing so much lately, working hard at school, and so often now it is Sonya who makes his dinner. He can't let her get behind in school. She has been doing so well. Her English is almost perfect.

If they had stayed in Bolivia, Sonya would not have gone to college. Maybe she would have married the son of Don Miguel Dimas, the owner of the coffee plantation. He was a nice boy; he wanted to be a doctor. Sonya had liked it there too. She was friends with everyone, and she ran around without shoes like all the other children. Margot was always scolding her about it, and he should have too so that she wouldn't have ended up with parasites like everyone else. He should have known better. He had known better, but he had not wanted her to feel like he felt, like a stranger.

He would have been a stranger even if he could have written down every word in the Spanish dictionary and known them all, even known their etymologies, written them all down in his leather-bound notebook that he had bought just before leaving Vienna because it was beautiful and he thought that maybe he would keep a diary of their flight, of his exile, his own personal account of the war years. It would have been something for his grandchildren to read. Instead he had started writing down all the words he didn't know, and the list had grown longer and longer. He knew from the start that he would never become part of Bolivia, of that earth that smelled so strongly of soil it was as if it were alive. And it was alive—with insects and fat worms and water-laden, rubbery plants. No matter how much he tried—and he did try, wearing rope sandals and baggy white linen pants and a Panama hat—he was a stranger. He would like to have that hat with him now; he would like to feel its stiffness on his head. But the hat is lost, and he does not even remember when he lost it.

Even the priest, who was so alone, so far away from everyone and everything, was part of the red earth and the rain, part of the noise of the thousands of insects in his garden. The priest was addicted to opium, but he had no desire to give up his habit, so after a while they stopped talking about it. The priest had only called for a doctor as a matter of protocol. It wasn't right, even at the edge of the Amazon, even in *godforsaken Rurrenabaque*, as the priest called it, for a priest to be an addict. An alcoholic, that was understandable, but not an addict. And he drank too. That made it worse.

After their first meeting, Karl returned often to visit the priest. They sat on the cool cane chairs on the priest's veranda. Sometimes they hardly spoke at all. They sat on the veranda and drank Irish whiskey, which the priest ordered especially from the capital once a month. They sat on the veranda and drank Irish whiskey and listened to records on the priest's old Victrola. They liked the same music, Bach especially. Sometimes they would listen to the entire *Magnificat* without speaking a word, hardly moving except to drink. The priest found Karl's love for the *Magnificat* amusing. "After all, you are a Jew," he would say.

"But so was Christ," Karl would reply, and the priest would shake his head.

Once the priest had said, "You have been sent to me by God to relieve me of my own thoughts. I have had conversations with only myself for so many years that I had nearly forgotten that there were people to talk to, not just people who list their sins and ask for forgiveness. And who am I to grant forgiveness?"

At first Karl had felt strange being a priest's friend, but after a while he almost forgot that his friend was a priest, though Karl would sometimes ask him to recite the Latin prayers because they both loved that dead language, and sometimes they would speak in Latin and it was like the secret talk of schoolchildren. Karl always came home from an afternoon with the priest invigorated, filled with ideas that made him want to write books. But whenever he sat at his desk with a blank sheet of paper in front of him, pen in hand, his ideas suddenly became mere banalities. He had wanted to write a book of dialogues between him and the priest, like Plato. But those conversations were part of a private world, mixed inextricably with the humid smells of the jungle and noises from strange birds and screeching monkeys and insects. He could never find a way to put the priest's glazed and staring eyes into words. They were eyes that had spent hours watching a crack in the wall slink and curl about like a snake.

Once, Karl invited the priest for dinner, and he told Margot to be kind because the priest was a sick man and unused to socializing. Later, his wife said that she was afraid of the priest's eyes. She said they were like the eyes of a dead fish, more alive than dead, and yet one knows they are dead.

After the dinner, the priest told Karl, "Your wife is very beautiful and very unhappy." How well he understood things. Was it the drugs and the long nights on the veranda just watching the mosquitoes around the naked lightbulb? "It has been many years since I have been with a woman," the priest continued. "That is because I am weak and selfish and not because I am a priest. I am a priest because I am unable to love. I could have been a general, too, but I dislike pomp and cannot have enemies. I cannot hate, either."

At first these confessions made Karl nervous because he thought that he had to say something, but he could never think of anything to say, and later he realized that that was why the priest told him things—because he offered neither advice nor consolation. They both understood that there was nothing anyone could do or say, so Karl began telling the priest things too. "My wife tried to kill herself yesterday," Karl said. "I came home and she was lying on the kitchen floor, blood streaming out of her wrists. I don't know whether she was glad that I saved her or whether she was sorry."

Now Karl remembers the priest's reply: "Sometimes I think of killing myself."

Perhaps it was the heat and the sun and the afternoon torrents of rain that made it impossible for the priest to kill himself cleanly and quickly. Or perhaps it was a combination of pride and revenge and also—though the priest would never admit it—a glimmer of love for his miserable town with its hunched houses clustered together around his crumbling, whitewashed church. In any case, he preferred the slow, wasting-away path of drugs and loneliness.

The only thing that Karl did not understand about the priest was that he didn't care about the war. He never read the papers and would become restless when Karl ran up the steps to the veranda waving a newspaper and began reading to him excitedly about the latest Allied victory. Throughout their stay in Bolivia, Karl still dreamed of going back to Vienna when it was all over. He did not know then that when it was all over and they released the photographs of the living corpses with shaved heads, grasping at barbed-wire fences with bone hands, he and Margot would no longer want to return to that ghost-filled city.

The priest used to say that war was not important, and it would make Karl want to clench his hands around the priest's neck and shake him until he could see how important it was that thousands, maybe even millions, of people were dying in Europe. At the end, when he showed the priest the photographs from the concentration camps, the priest only shook his head and drank from his glass.

And now, at the end of another day, with the fifteen blocks in the cold still ahead, he thinks that maybe the priest was right. Maybe war is not that important. Because what has really changed? Margot is the same as she always has been—in Vienna, in Rurrenabaque, and now in New York. It has always been too much for her to see the sun shining through the lace curtains or to kiss her daughter good-bye in the morning. He would like to take all the shiny, sterilized instruments that the nurse laid out so carefully on the white cloth on his instrument table and throw them from the window, let them fall into the dirty alley below and mingle with the rats and wet newspapers, the cigarette butts, and discarded, rusting cans.

He could go to the movies. It would be warm there and he could slump down in his seat so only the top of his head would be visible from behind, and he could stretch his legs and allow himself to be taken somewhere else. But by the time the movie was over, it would be even darker and even colder, and Margot would be worried because he is never that late.

He gets up slowly from his chair and stretches. His foot has fallen asleep, and he stamps it absentmindedly on the floor while he puts the *Herald Tribune* into his briefcase. He walks through his office very slowly with his hat and gloves already on and his coat all buttoned up and his scarf neatly tucked into his collar. He turns on the light in the examination room, just to make sure everything is in order. He turns it off. He checks his office once more, but instead of leaving, he falls back into his chair and closes his eyes.

He can feel the jungle coming back again. He can almost smell the sweat on his body and the whiskey in his glass. It is an unusually hot night. He can feel the beads of sweat forming on his forehead. Soon they will start to trickle down into his eyes. He wipes his forehead with his hand. He drinks from his glass. The whiskey burns his throat and sends a chill down his spine despite the heat. It is time to go home, but still he is lingering in the cane chair on the veranda. *Just one more record, one more whiskey, one more cigar*, he tells himself. It is too hot to move anyway, and it is a long walk home along the overgrown path. He has never stayed at the priest's so long. He is afraid to look at his watch because he knows he is later than he has ever been before. If there were a phone, he would call, but only Don Miguel Dimas and the mayor have a phone.

"I should be going, Antonio," Karl says, and the priest nods. But Karl stays in his chair. *Just a few more minutes. It is already so late, a few minutes won't make any difference*, he thinks. Antonio lights a cigarette, and Karl sees in the flame's glow the blurred outline of his thin lips. The glow intensifies as he inhales. They sit in silence for a long time. The priest finishes his cigarette and lights another one. The record is over, but neither of them stands up to lift the needle, so the sound of scratching blends in with the other night noises—the insects, the monkeys, the heavy plants rubbing against each other in the hot breeze.

After a long while, he hears Antonio say from the other side of the veranda, "You could stay here tonight, Karl. It's too late to go back."

"No," Karl says. "I have to get back." And with a tremendous effort he rises from his chair and walks down the steps toward the path. "Good-bye," he calls.

Now the wind is lashing his face and he can feel his skin reddening and he has to hold his hat on with his hand. He hardly passes anyone on the walk home, just a few bundled-up figures, battling the wind and cold. He comes to his building. He looks up and stares briefly at the light in his apartment. He enters the building and climbs the stairs to the fourth floor. He puts his ear to the door and listens. He can hear the radio. That is a good sign. He puts the key in the lock and turns it slowly, quietly. Something smells good. The *Appassionata* is playing. He hums along with it as he removes his gloves and hat and hangs up his coat.

It is too hot in the apartment. It is always too hot, no matter how cold it is outside. He can almost feel the steam spewing out of the radiator, filling the room with a wet, musty smell. He remembers coming in from the hot sun in Rurrenabaque. It was always so much cooler inside their house. If he were there now, he would take his shoes off and feel the rough mats beneath his feet, but he does not take his shoes off in New York, not until it is time to go to bed.

Only a dim lamp is on in the living room. It throws a brownish glow onto the heavy, new sofa. Almost everything in the apartment is new. They left their tiny Bolivian house almost completely intact. They did not take the thin, colorful blankets or the mosquito nets. He had wanted to take the mosquito nets—they had been such a comfort—but Margot had laughed. And she had been right. There would be no need for them in New York.

Karl is afraid he will not be able to get up if he sits down in one of the deep armchairs. He wonders how they ended up with all this heavy furniture—the long oak table with the four high-backed chairs, the floor lamps, the sofa.

He sits uncomfortably at the edge of the sofa. He is so tired. He is so tired that he isn't even hungry, though he had been so busy that he didn't have a chance to each lunch. He could use some whiskey, but they don't keep any liquor in the house. He has gotten out of the habit of drinking. Instead, there are countless cups of coffee with heavy cream.

When they were all packed and they had their bus tickets to Lima, Karl went to visit the priest one last time.

"We're leaving tomorrow," he said.

"I know."

"How did you know?"

"I am the priest, Karl. People tell me everything." And the priest had laughed. Then he poured Karl some whiskey, and they sat there as they had been sitting for six years. Karl shook his head. *Six years is a long time*, he thought, but he did not speak.

It grew dark, and Karl could not bring himself to speak, and it was getting late, so he got up from his chair, and the cane creaked as it relieved itself of its burden.

"Good-bye," they said, and they shook hands. It almost made Karl laugh, that shaking of hands. After six years, it seemed like such a meager gesture. They did not promise to write. And they hadn't written. *What*, Karl thinks, *could he have written?* It would all sound so stupid.

And now it is almost impossible for him to get up from the couch. But he has no choice. He walks slowly down the hall to their bedroom. The door is closed, but the light is on. He pushes the door open. Margot is lying on the bed, propped up on two pillows, reading a magazine. She looks up and smiles. "I didn't hear you come in," she says.

"I hope you weren't worried."

"No, I was resting." Since there is nothing to say, he goes to the bed and lies down next to her. And as he buries his face in the warmth of her sweater that smells, very faintly, of mothballs, he remembers what the priest had said: "Your wife is very beautiful and very unhappy."

the buchovskys on their own

Until the day he left for the Soviet Union, Isaac had never spent a full night away from his daughters. Simone was in the seventh and Juliet in the fifth grade when he made the decision to leave them on their own. Of course he did not leave them completely on their own, but in his mind, and in theirs too, on their own meant without him. He had put off his journey to the Soviet Union as long as possible, but his work required it as there were documents and manuscripts there that he needed to examine. Isaac was writing a book on the role of assimilated Jews in prerevolutionary Russia and had exhausted the information available in the New York Public Library and all the major libraries on the East Coast. He had gone to a great deal of trouble to get permission and grants to spend this month in the Soviet Union, and he had to go through with it or the book would never be written. He explained this in great detail to his daughters, who were very understanding about the whole thing. In fact, though they did not tell him so, they half looked forward to being on their own, even if it wasn't completely on their own, though they would, of course, think of him often, imagining him sitting at an old library table in a dusty corner of an unused library reading the almost-illegible scrawl of people who were no longer alive. They wondered whether their father's hotel room would be bugged and whether secret agents would follow him around.

Katja Ladijinskaya, whom they always called Katja Ladijinskaya, never just Katja or Miss Ladijinskaya, was a childhood friend of their father and was really the only person Isaac knew well enough to ask to stay with the girls. Her parents and Isaac's parents had known each other in Russia and had lived in exile together, first in Berlin and then in Paris. They had all come over to New York on the same boat from Lisbon in 1941, and so they were as close to being brother and sister as they could be without really being brother and sister at all. Still, despite the connection between their families, Isaac had been hesitant to ask for her help, though Katja Ladijinskaya was not at all hesitant to accept the responsibility. In fact, she claimed that she was quite looking forward to spending more time with Simone and Juliet and, she added, a month in the country would do her good, although Tenafly, New Jersey, was hardly the country, and her daily commute to the Upper East Side would surely be tedious. She lived alone in a large apartment on 106th Street and Riverside Drive and taught French at a prestigious private high school to whose students she was fiercely devoted, despite the fact that they were all, according to her, "spoiled Philistines." Still, her students loved her and called her *The Jin*. Katja Ladijinskaya spent her summers in Paris secretly counting the days until the school year started again.

Katja Ladijinskaya's favorite color was aubergine. She always wore at least one article of clothing of that color. She had an aubergine beret of which she was very fond and plenty of aubergine scarves. Simone and Juliet liked Katja Ladijinskaya, but they were not always sure how to behave around her and were somewhat worried about how their life together would turn out. Although they were by no stretch of the imagination noisy children, they worried that they would be too noisy for Katja Ladijinskaya, who was used to older girls. They still remembered very clearly how on Thanksgiving Day two years before she had referred to the music they were playing on the phonograph upstairs as *pure drivel*. It was the month when they played the song "Which Way You Goin' Billy?" by the Poppy Family at least five times a day. Katja Ladijinskaya had wandered upstairs to see what they were up to. She had knocked on the door and they had invited her in and she had sat with them on the floor all dressed up in black velvet pants, black suede shoes, an aubergine satin blouse, and a black crepe scarf and listened to the record with them. Then she proclaimed that the music was *pure drivel* and wanted to hear another one of their records, but instead they showed her some of their drawings, which she found charming.

Katja Ladijinskaya arrived on the last bus the night before their father left. Simone and Juliet were already in bed, but when they heard the bus stop, they went to the window to watch her as she stood across the street holding her blue Samsonite suitcase, waiting for a chance to cross. In the morning they awoke to the sounds of Katja Ladijinskaya and their father talking in the kitchen rather than to the usual sounds of the classical music radio station. Katja Ladijinskaya would not allow their father to help her prepare breakfast—she had brought brioches and black currant preserve from New York. "I do not want to shirk my responsibilities," she insisted when their father tried to put the coffee on. Later, when they were helping their father pack his toiletry bag, they asked if Katja Ladijinskaya was being paid to stay with them.

"Paid? Why would you think that? She is a very old friend," their father said.

"She said she didn't want to shirk her responsibilities," Simone explained.

"That's just the way she is. She's always been very industrious. When we were children and I was being lazy about somcthing, my mother would always say, 'Why can't you be industrious like our Katja?'"

It was flurrying when the airport limousine pulled out of the driveway. They all waved to Isaac, who, despite his height, almost seemed small in the backseat of such a large vehicle. "Leningrad is at its most beautiful in the spring. Too bad your father couldn't wait until spring," Katja Ladinjinska said as the three of them stood in the doorway looking out at the empty driveway.

"I hate the spring," Juliet said.

"How is it possible to hate a season? One should never use such a word flippantly."

"She always says she hates things. She doesn't really mean it," Simone said, coming to her sister's aid.

"Well, if she doesn't really mean it, she shouldn't say it," Katja Kadijinska replied.

"But I do mean it. Spring makes me tired and I hate being tired."

"Well, at least you have a reason," Katja Ladijinskaya said. "Let's make some coffee." And though they didn't really like coffee, they drank coffee with Katja Ladijinskaya and found it quite pleasant, sitting in the dining room, watching the flurries, drinking bitter, black coffee with no sugar or milk.

Going through customs was easier than Isaac had imagined. The young soldiers opened all three of his oversized suitcases and rifled distractedly through their contents. They did not ask him why he had nine children's snowsuits and twenty packages of pantyhose. They simply slipped the packs of Marlboros and

Winstons that he had scattered throughout the suitcases into their pockets or under the counter without a word, just as his colleagues who had already made the trip to the Soviet Union had told him they would do.

He and his parents had left when he was barely three years old, so he had no memories of the Soviet Union at all, but he hoped, at the very least, to feel some swell of emotion upon finally returning to the country of his birth. Russian, as his parents never let him forget, was his mother tongue, despite the fact that both his tongue and his pen preferred French or English. But when he arrived, he was disappointed by the lack of snow. He had been expecting everything to be white. Instead, all he saw was gray and brown—gray buildings and gray roads, brown hats, brown coats, polluted, brown skies—so that he felt the weight of those two colors on him like a heavy but not so warm blanket.

On the way from the airport, he and the taxi driver did not talk except to confirm the name of his hotel. Isaac did not want to make the man nervous by engaging in chitchat, asking about his family, his lunch. All that could lead to trouble. He had been told that people preferred not to talk to foreigners. He was prepared for that, prepared for the fact that his relatives, whom he had never met, might not want to see him. Still, just in case, he had brought photographs of his parents and his daughters as well as the snowsuits and pantyhose, blue jeans, and Palmolive soap and Bayer aspirin. He was worried that the snowsuits would be too bright, that the children would be embarrassed to wear yellow or red or blue, though he knew that children did not worry about such things.

"Do you have a hat?" the taxi driver asked him as he lifted the three large suitcases out of the trunk.

"No, I am not accustomed to wearing a hat," Isaac said.

"Here in Leningrad the winter is very cold," the driver said as if he thought Isaac had never experienced winter. "You must buy a hat." The taxi driver was the first of dozens to be concerned about his lack of headgear, though the others were all old women. These women were relentless, accosting him on the street with their grave warnings about the horrors of frostbite.

"Look," he told one old woman. "There's not even any snow on the ground."

"Just wait," the woman said. "Just wait."

After that, he almost gave in and bought a woolen cap, but at the last minute he changed his mind. He would not, he decided, be bullied into headgear by old women.

Although the hat obsession was certainly tiresome, what frustrated him most was the waiting. Of course, he had known about the lines for buying food. Everyone knew about those. But he had no way of knowing what the waiting really meant, how it could affect you, eat into you like a brain-consuming worm until you became lethargy itself. He waited for his breakfast and for his lunch and for his dinner, and each meal involved several layers of waiting. First he waited for the waiter to bring the menu. This could take up to one hour, despite his vigorous requests and gestures. Then he waited for the waiter to take his order. Even such a simple thing took some time because they had to go through the entire leather-bound menu until he happened upon the only available dish, the pork cutlet or cabbage soup that was actually the only food being prepared that day. Once he tried asking the waiter what was actually available that day, but the waiter merely nodded at the menu, and they had to go through the whole sham the way they always did until he hit on the right answer. After the ordering was completed, he waited for the food to arrive, which was by far the longest part of the process and could take up to two hours if the restaurant staff were so inclined. Finally, there was a good half-hour wait until the waiter brought him the check. After the first few days he had to give up both breakfast and lunch because, given the erratic schedule at the library, eating could easily take up most of his valuable archive time.

He had also waited for days before he was finally granted permission to enter the archives, even though he had been told that this was already arranged and had been given a thick folder of signed and sealed papers to prove it. On the first day that he actually gained access to the archives, he arrived promptly at nine but ended up waiting for two hours until an old woman with a large ring of keys walked up to the door and took her time turning the key in the lock. "Wait," she told him gruffly as he tried to follow her inside. The door slammed, and it was another thirty minutes before he was allowed to enter.

He never knew when the archives would open though the sign on the door very clearly said, *Archive Hours 9–5:30, Monday–Saturday*. Sometimes they opened at ten, sometimes at nine thirty, sometimes at eleven, but never at nine. He also never knew when they would close, but usually at about three, maybe three thirty, the woman told him that it was time for him to pack up his things. Once—perhaps she had fallen asleep—it was almost seven before she told him she was closing up.

Because he had no time to spend on breakfast and lunch, he was ravenous by the time he ate his dinner, which he always had in the hotel restaurant since there were no restaurants really except for hotel restaurants. He thought sometimes of trying out another hotel restaurant to see whether it was more efficient, but he was always too debilitated by the end of a long day with no food for such experiments.

In the morning, instead of eating breakfast, he ran. He thought he would call a great deal of attention to himself with his running because exercise of this type was certainly not popular among the Soviets, but he soon found that no one seemed to pay him any attention. In the mornings, he noticed, people were quiet and slow as if they were still dreaming in their warm beds. It was after dark that the old women scolded him about not having a hat.

As far as he knew, there were only three other guests at the hotel during his entire two-month stay. There were two portly Romanians, who, whenever he passed them on the stairway or in the lobby, switched from Romanian to very loud and heavily accented French.

"*Bonjour, Monsieur*," they said to him.

Isaac would bow slightly and reply, "*Bonjour, Messieurs*." He did not know what their business in Leningrad was.

The other guest was a handsome African who always wore traditional African clothing and inquired in English after Isaac's health and the health of his family each time they met.

"And your family is well?" he would ask, and Isaac would answer, "Yes, very well, and yours?"

"Very well," the African would say.

Of course he missed the girls. He worried about how they were getting along with Katja Ladijinskaya, who was not always easy to get along with. Still, he found a rhythm to his days and was content to immerse himself in the lives of people who had died before he was born. There was safety in knowing that their lives would never touch his, that he could learn the intimate details of their business anxieties or troubles with the authorities, yet they would never demand anything of him in return.

On Sundays the archives were closed, so Isaac walked. He walked from one end of Leningrad to the other. Then he would write the girls a long letter about what he had seen. He put off calling his relatives.

Juliet realized after the second day that Katja Ladijinskaya wasn't really, as she and Simone had suspected, a snob at all. She was just shy. It was Juliet who noticed that her fingernails were bitten down almost to the moons and that she didn't look them straight in the eyes when she asked them whether they wanted more soup or what they had done at school. It took a day or so to convince Simone of her theory because Simone was going through a phase when she thought absolutely everyone was a snob. "Is Miss Dougherty a snob?" Juliet had asked because if anyone wasn't a snob, it was Miss Dougherty, the gym teacher. She wore the same white shorts and red T-shirt every day and smelled of old sneakers and boxed-up sweat. Simone said that she was a snob of sorts.

"What is a snob of sorts?" Juliet asked.

"Everyone is a snob about something even if they're not a typical snob."

"How about our father? Is he a snob?"

"That's not fair," Simone said.

"What's not fair about it? You said everyone is a snob or a snob of sorts."

"Everyone except us," Simone said.

"Oh. Well, isn't Katja Ladijinskaya one of us?'

Simone shrugged.

But Katja Ladijinskaya was one of them. Juliet knew it. After a few more days, Simone came around, and after showering from her daily afternoon run, Simone too started hanging around the kitchen while Katja Ladijinskaya made dinner, which was always fish. Luckily Simone and Juliet both liked fish. Katja Ladijinskaya bought it fresh every afternoon at the fishmonger's (her word) next to her school. This particular fishmonger, she assured them, had the best selection of fish in Manhattan. She brought home Pacific fish and Atlantic fish, river fish and lake fish. Some nights she broiled and others she sautéed. Every once in a while she baked the fish, but their favorite was sautéed because of the sauces. Katja Ladijinskaya told them that when she was young, she had wanted to be a chef, but in those days women did not become chefs. "The French are misogynists," she explained.

"What's a misogynist?" Juliet asked, and Katja Ladijinskaya told her to look it up in the dictionary.

"You'll remember it better if you look it up yourself," she said.

"A misogynist is someone who hates women," Simone said proudly.

"Showing off does not suit you," Katja Ladijinskaya said sternly, shaking her head as she squeezed lemon over the sea bass.

At dinner they were expected to speak French, which meant that Katja Ladijinskaya did most of the talking and Simone and Juliet had to concentrate so hard to understand more or less what she was saying that they ate excruciatingly slowly, and Katja Ladijinskaya was always telling them that their fish was getting cold, not to mention the vegetables. One evening Juliet tried smiling a lot and nodding her head instead of listening, but it made her feel too sad to be fooling Katja Ladijinskaya, so she started listening again.

After dinner Juliet and Simone cleaned up and Katja Ladijinskaya meticulously corrected papers, muttering and sighing over each one in a quiet, patient way, carefully writing long comments in minuscule print in the margins. When they finished the dishes, the girls were allowed to do their homework at the dining room table also. Katja Ladijinskaya never asked to check their progress or to see what they were working on, but she seemed to like their presence and would look up at them every once in a while and smile. At nine they were sent to bed, but they were permitted to read for as long as they wished.

On many nights Katja Ladijinskaya made a telephone call. She whispered in Russian (even though the girls did not understand Russian) for at least half an hour, usually more. Sometimes during her conversation she would laugh and sometimes she wouldn't. Sometimes she talked a lot and other times she listened more than she talked.

"Who do you call every night?" Juliet asked her one evening.

"Whom," Katja Ladijinskaya said.

"Okay, *whom* do you call every night?"

"A friend," she said. Once they lifted the receiver on the telephone in their father's bedroom quietly and listened to Katja Ladijinskaya and her friend talking. Her friend's voice was raspy, but when she laughed there was no trace of raspiness at all.

On the fourth night, when they were already sufficiently tired out from speaking French, they asked Katja Ladijinskaya if she could teach them Russian.

"Why on earth would you want to learn Russian?"

"It sounds nice," Juliet said.

"That's not a very good reason," Katja Ladijinskaya answered.

"There are so many great Russian authors, and when we visit some of our father's friends, we never know what's going on, which is both embarrassing and boring," Simone said in her most adult tone.

"French is far more useful than Russian, and your father agrees with me."

"French is stupid," Juliet said, but Katja Ladijinskaya ignored her. "Everyone speaks French," she added, trying to be more rational, but Katja Ladijinskaya was done with the conversation.

On the second Saturday morning of their father's absence, they were told to pack a few things, including something *festive*, because they were going to spend the weekend in New York at Katja Ladijinskaya's apartment. On the bus ride there they discussed the fact that they had never slept in the city before, and Katja Ladijinskaya said she always found it difficult to sleep without the sound of traffic.

Her corner apartment was a two-bedroom with a long corridor. From the living room one could see the Hudson River, but the bedrooms faced 106th Street. Juliet and Simone thought they should have made the bedrooms facing the river because it would have been nice to wake up in the morning and see the river first thing. The walls of Katja Ladijinskaya's apartment were lined with bookshelves, and in the spaces that were not taken up by books were paintings of Paris by Katja Ladijinskaya's late mother. A photograph of her mother wearing a long flowing gown posing in front of one of her larger paintings—a mother and daughter on a park bench—hung over the dining room table. A few years earlier, Katja Ladijinskaya had told them that the paintings were not very good. Simone and Juliet had spent that afternoon, after a long and filling lunch, examining all the paintings, unsuccessfully looking for flaws while Katja Ladijinskaya and their father drank countless cups of tea and spoke in French about boring things, but they never asked Katja Ladijinskaya to point out what was wrong with the paintings because they knew she would raise her eyebrows and tell them that was because they were not looking properly.

After they had been shown their room and Katja Ladijinskaya had instructed them to keep themselves occupied while she went out to do some errands—insisting that food shopping was not a constructive activity and that all three of them should not waste their time with it—they examined the paintings again.

"Do you think it's the colors?" Juliet said.

"What do you mean, the colors?"

"I mean that they're ugly—all those pinks and mint green and pale yellow. Don't you think they're ugly?"

"Colors aren't ugly by nature," Simone said.

"Combinations of colors can be ugly by nature," Juliet said, realizing that she had gotten to the crux of it.

"I guess. I wonder why she keeps them up if they're so bad," Simone said.

"I guess she liked her mother," Juliet said.

"I guess."

When they were very little, Katja Ladijinskaya's mother used to sit by the window and look out at the river. She didn't speak to them, but she talked to their father as if he were still a child. "Isaac," she would say, "you must be careful on your bicycle." Sometimes she would look at Simone and Juliet and ask her daughter who they were, and Katja Ladijinskaya would say that they were the neighbor's children, but then she would ask the same question again a few minutes later. Their father had explained to them that she was ill, that she had lost her mind during the war.

Katja Ladijinskaya came back with the groceries. "It's beastly hot in here," she said, flinging open all the windows so the wind from the Hudson blew papers around the living room, but Katja Ladijinskaya did not pick them up. She put on Vladimir Horowitz playing Chopin as loud as it could go and told them to occupy themselves while she prepared lunch. "Too many cooks spoil the broth," she said when they asked if they could help.

"Can we go running?" Simone asked.

"Must you?" Katja Ladijinskaya said. They tried to read but the music was too loud, so they danced—flailing their arms around as if they were drunk, prancing with tiny little steps around and around the living room, writhing on the ground and up again, back to the tiny steps and then long leaps and spinning, spinning, spinning. They would have preferred running. Then the music stopped and Katja Ladijinskaya ran to them, bent down, and put her heavy arms around their shoulders. "My children, it is time to get dressed," she said. Her hair smelled of salmon.

They had all been sitting properly in the living room in their *festive* clothes for about fifteen minutes when the doorbell rang. Katja Ladijinskaya rose slowly, flinging an unusually long gold and aubergine silk scarf over her shoulder as she walked to the door. "My name is Alexandra," said their guest, a small, thin woman with short blond hair and very green eyes. They recognized her voice from the phone and were surprised that it came from such a small, almost frail body. They all shook hands. Juliet and Simone mumbled their names, and Katja Ladijinskaya told them not to mumble, to look at their "interlocutor," which they did. She was dressed all in black except for a yellow beret, which she did not remove when they took her coat. This was the first time that an adult had introduced herself to them with only a first name, and they felt quite proud although a little shy about having to use it.

At lunch they were each given a small glass of undiluted white wine because Alexandra said it was "a sin to add water to ambrosia." "So," Alexandra turned to them, "I hear your father is on a sojourn behind the Iron Curtain."

"Yes, he is. He's doing research in Leningrad."

"Does he really call it Leningrad? I'm surprised." Alexandra directed this question to Katja Ladijinskaya.

"Isaac is not a Romantic," Katja Ladijinskaya answered.

"It's not a question of whether he's a Romantic or not. It's a question of principle, don't you think?" She turned to Simone.

Of course Simone knew that Leningrad used to be St. Petersburg and that there were many people who refused to acknowledge the name change. She knew why that could be a matter of principle, but she wasn't sure about why her father wasn't a Romantic, or what a Romantic was, even though she was fairly sure he wasn't one. It didn't seem like something he would be. Alexandra took a sip of wine and waited for Simone to respond. Juliet giggled. "Yes, it is a matter of principle," Simone answered gravely.

"You see," Alexandra said.

Katja Ladijinskaya laughed and said, "Don't be absurd, Alya."

"I'm not being absurd. It is a question of principle. I would like to say that I would rather die than call Petersburg Leningrad, but that would be an exaggeration, so I won't say it."

"Are you a Romantic?" Juliet asked.

"I don't know." Alexandra looked back at Juliet very seriously. "I'd like to think so, but I'm afraid I'm not. And how about you?"

"Oh, I'm too young," Juliet said, and Katja and Alexandra and Juliet laughed.

"You're too young and I'm too old," Alexandra said, although she seemed quite a bit younger than Katja Ladijinskaya.

After the soup, Katja Ladijinskaya brought out the salmon, which Alexandra had to tell her was perfect at least three times because Katja Ladijinskaya kept saying that she thought it was a little dry. Simone ended up having thirds because Alexandra could only eat one helping and she could tell that Katja Ladijinskaya didn't believe she had liked the fish, even though Simone knew that Alexandra was the type of person who never ate more than one serving of anything.

After lunch they went for a walk in Riverside Park. Simone and Juliet wanted to change into pants, but Katja Ladijinskaya insisted that they remain *properly attired*. Alexandra raised her eyebrows but didn't say anything.

Katja Ladijinskaya and Alexandra walked at a snail's pace, stopping to point out perfectly ordinary birds, mainly pigeons, and to watch squirrels clambering up trees. Sometimes they gazed out at the river without speaking. Simone and Juliet tried running ahead only to be called back and told that it was not good to run after a heavy meal. Their legs, clad in thin tights, got cold and itchy. They tried not to look at the street signs because that only highlighted their slow progress. Finally, when their faces and ears had turned to ice and they could no longer feel their feet, Katja Ladijinskaya and Alexandra headed inland toward Broadway and a warm coffee shop.

"Are you sure you want hot chocolate?" Katja Ladijinskaya asked them two times before she reluctantly agreed to let them order it.

"What's wrong with hot chocolate?" Juliet asked because she had never encountered such opposition to it before.

"Nothing at all. Hot chocolate is a perfectly fine afternoon beverage and you shouldn't let Katja give you a complex about it," Alexandra said.

"What's a complex?" Juliet asked.

"It's when you feel inferior about something," Alexandra answered.

"How can hot chocolate make you feel inferior?" Juliet persisted.

"It can't. That's the point," Simone said to put an end to the conversation. During this entire interchange Katja Ladijinskaya was looking at Alexandra as if she were trying to remember something very important she wanted to tell her, but couldn't. Then the waitress came to take the order.

"No one wants a little something sweet?" Katja Ladijinskaya asked, and no one did.

"You order something, if you want," Alexandra said, but Katja Ladijinskaya just ordered tea. Then there was a discussion about whether to take the bus or the subway home. Simone and Juliet campaigned for the subway because they liked standing in the first car and watching the train make its way through the tunnel. As it turned out, the bus was right there when they walked out of the restaurant, which was, according to both Katja Ladijinskaya and Alexandra, a *stroke of luck*.

When they got back to the apartment, Katja Ladijinskaya said it was time to take a nap, but Juliet and Simone weren't tired at all and asked if they could play on the elevator instead. This suggestion was met with shock on the part of both Alexandra and Katja Ladijinskaya, who explained that elevators were not toys and should not be used unnecessarily as such abuse would weaken the chains, putting all elevator riders at risk. "Imagine if a nice family plummeted to their deaths," Alexandra said, and Juliet and Simone tried to imagine a nice family riding innocently in the elevator when *ploof*, down they would go. Later when they were in their room taking their *nap*, they talked about it and agreed that it was not a sure fact that a crash would necessarily mean death. It all depended upon from which floor the occupants fell and whether they had had the presence of mind to shield their heads. In the end, they decided that the elevators were much safer than Katja Ladijinskaya and Alexandra thought and that they could have played on them without putting anyone in harm's way. It was, after all, a rather large building with a lot of people who came and went. The elevators were probably running day and night anyway.

After they talked about elevators, they jumped on the bed for a while, but they had a hard time keeping quiet, so they had to give up that activity. They read and played a game of chess and read some more, and then they were hungry. They realized it had been dark for quite some time, so they tiptoed out into the hall to see if there was any activity at all in the rest of the apartment. Everything was dark. There was no light shining from under the doorway to Katja Ladijinskaya's room.

Finally, they crept into the kitchen in their stocking feet and prepared themselves thick slices of bread with butter and buckwheat honey, which they brought back to their rooms and ate sitting on the bed. After their dinner they looked out the window and watched people walking up and down 106th Street, and then they played Concentration, laying the cards out on the bed. When they felt it was time to go to sleep, they tiptoed to the bathroom and brushed their teeth and washed their faces. There was still no light on in Katja Ladijinskaya's room, but they thought they heard whispering although they did not feel right about putting their ears to the door to find out for sure.

In the morning, Katja Ladijinskaya whistled the entire time she was preparing the spinach omelet for their breakfast. She didn't whistle any particular tune, at least not one that they could recognize. It was more like the same note over and over again, faster and faster and faster.

"Alexandra had to leave quite unexpectedly," Katja Ladijinskaya announced as they sat down to eat. "She asked me to say goodbye and to tell you that she very much enjoyed your company."

"Are we going home after breakfast?" Juliet asked.

Katja Ladijinskaya didn't answer. She cut a piece of her omelet, put it in her mouth and chewed, looking straight ahead, right through them.

Katja Ladijinskaya started crying. Tears rolled down her cheeks and she put down her knife and fork. She made no effort to dry her tears or to speak. She simply sat at the table and cried. Finally, Simone got up and stood next to her, so Juliet got up too and stood on the other side of her, and just as suddenly as Katja Ladijinskaya had started crying, she stopped. "Don't do what I have done," she whispered, and then she started crying again. And they said they wouldn't, which only made her cry more, so they didn't ask her what it was she had done. Juliet knew she had heard that phrase before but couldn't place it until a few days later when she remembered that it was in the song "The House of the Rising Sun," which she didn't understand but liked anyway. She wondered whether Katja Ladijinskaya had ever heard the song and if she had, whether she thought it was drivel, but she never asked her.

Katja Ladijinskaya stopped crying again, just as abruptly as she had the first time. Very calmly she said, "We can go back to New Jersey whenever it suits you."

"I was just asking," Juliet said.

"Maybe we could go to the museum first," Simone suggested even though she didn't really feel like going to a museum. She would have liked to run from one tip of Manhattan to the other, but that, she knew, was out of the question.

"As you like," Katja Ladijinskaya said, so they took the hot, crowded bus to the Met, where they walked aimlessly through the Egyptian rooms. Then they were back on the hot bus again on their way to the Port Authority Bus Station, where they would take another hot bus home.

On Monday they went back to their regular routine, only Katja Ladijinskaya didn't bring home any more fish. After that weekend they ate a lot of scrambled eggs and frozen spinach and broiled chicken and lots of Lipton and Campbell Soup—tomato and chicken noodle and pea. Pea soup was their favorite. On some nights when Katja Ladijinskaya said, "My children, I don't think I could bear to cook tonight," Simone and Juliet made plain rice with butter and salt and served this austere meal to Katja Ladijinskaya, who ate obediently and in silence, repairing to her bedroom immediately afterward. On those nights they also brought her chamomile tea in bed, and she would thank them and act as if she really didn't need so much pampering, but sometimes she would let them sit with her while she drank her tea, and when she was finished, she would thank them and order them to "leave an old woman alone." She looked very large in the bed, so much larger than their father looked when he was lying in bed, his head propped up on two big pillows. The pillows made him look especially thin, but Katja Ladijinskaya made the pillows look small. Her arms, splayed out and unclothed, were as thick as thighs.

During this second half of their father's absence, Simone and Juliet were often afraid that they might wake up one morning to find Katja Ladijinskaya dead. On one level they knew this was not a rational fear because, though Katja Ladijinskaya called herself an old woman, she was, in fact, only two years older than their father, who was not old at all. Still, they worried and thought of calling their father in the Soviet Union to get his advice, but they did not know how to go about calling the Soviet Union. They knew that one had to call a special operator and then wait, sometimes for hours, for the call to go through. They could, of course, have figured it out if they had really wanted to, but their father did not believe in long-distance telephone calling unless it was an absolute emergency, and they were afraid he would not consider Katja Ladijinskaya's condition to be urgent enough to require a call to the other side of the Iron Curtain. Of course, they could have written to their father about what had happened to Katja Ladijinskaya, but instead they described in great detail what they were studying in school and enclosed in their letters charcoal self-portraits, which had to be folded extremely carefully so that they wouldn't smudge.

Isaac realized that he had been waiting for a snowstorm, that he thought somehow a snowstorm would make him realize that he really was in the Soviet Union, not just in a dusty library reading through the personal papers of minor intellectuals. He was sure that after it snowed he would call his relatives and they would invite him to their humble apartments, where they would drink plenty of vodka and eat good black bread and something special that they had waited in line for hours to acquire. They would talk about his parents and his grandparents. He would learn things about them that he had never known, and in the end, the children of his cousins and second cousins would don their new snowsuits and they would all walk back with him to his hotel in the snow.

It did snow, but instead of calling his relatives, he met Gita. Unbeknownst to him, the snow began as he sat in the windowless hall of the archives with his stacks of brittle paper and cardboard boxes. Instead of going directly back to the hotel and having his usual prolonged meal in the hotel restaurant, when he emerged from the archives and saw the snow, despite the growling in his stomach, he chose a walk over dinner. He walked without paying any attention to where he was going—turning abruptly onto small lanes when he felt moved to do so, walking in the middle of the large boulevards, which had become impassible to vehicles. Noisy groups of men invited him to join them for a drink. He wished them a joyous evening and continued on his way. Sometimes they ran after him, trying to convince him that there was nothing else he could possibly do that night that would be better than walking with them and drinking their vodka. "We have six bottles," one group of men said. He smiled and thanked them again but kept on walking.

Every once in a while he passed another lone walker, and they smiled at each other and continued on their ways. When he had walked for almost two hours, he realized that he was cold, so he looked around for a place to have tea or a piece of bread and cheese. But he was in a residential district and there was nothing. Still, he did not turn around. He was not ready to return to the hotel. And then he saw the lights—not hundreds of lights like at the opera, but to him it seemed like hundreds of lights—illuminating the first story of a large, square building. He climbed the stairs to the building and pulled on the massive iron doors. They opened. He had not expected them to open, but since they had, he walked in. Inside there was music. He followed the music and came upon a large hall filled with tables, at which were sitting men and women in brown suits. Everyone was enshrouded in cigarette smoke. At the end of the hall on a small stage was a string quartet playing a waltz. Above the stage was a banner that read, ACADEMY OF ARCHITECTS ANNUAL BANQUET. There was a dance floor, where half a dozen couples were dancing. The men whipped the women around much too forcefully, and the women laughed.

No one seemed to notice him in the doorway, so he walked in and stood in a corner. He grew braver and took an empty seat at a table whose occupants seemed particularly drunk. Someone offered him vodka and he accepted. He grabbed a piece of bread from the breadbasket and no one seemed to mind. Someone filled his glass again. One of the men at his table showed him a plaque he had been awarded for twenty years of service to architecture. "Congratulations," Isaac said, and everyone at the table clapped, and glasses were filled, and vodka was drunk. He ate what was left of the bread and announced that he was going to look for a dance partner. Someone slapped him on the back and off he went. He was actually going to leave, but the music stopped. A fat, important-looking man stepped onto the stage and started giving a speech about how architecture was the most glorious of socialist endeavors because it represented both the greatness of the socialist ideal and the strength and sweat of the Soviet worker. The man droned on. Isaac stopped listening, but he felt that it would be rude to leave during the speech. The members of the string quartet were sitting very straight and quietly in their chairs, but then the only woman in the group dropped her bow. Everyone ignored it except for him. He smiled at her, and she smiled back, and that was Gita.

He sat through the fat, important-looking man's speech and another speech by an even more important man and through the final toasts to architecture and the Soviet Union, to Lenin and Marx and a lot of people whose names were unfamiliar to him but who must have been members of the Academy of Architects because when their names were called, they stood up and bowed and everyone clapped. Then it was over, and the members of the string quartet packed up their instruments, and he followed Gita out the door into the snowy night.

"Excuse me," he called after her. At first she did not turn around although he knew she had heard him. "Miss," he tried again, and this time she turned.

"Yes?" she said, and then he didn't know what to say. She was about to turn back around when he noticed that she was not wearing a hat.

"You really should wear a hat in this weather," he said, and she laughed and told him that he should take his own advice, and that was how it started.

They walked for several hours, and when they were too tired to go on, she sneaked into the hotel with him. On that first night, the phone rang long after they had fallen asleep, though they had fallen asleep quite late. "Are you sure you are in the right place at the right time?" a voice said in heavily accented English.

"Excuse me?" Isaac answered in Russian, but the man had already hung up.

He told Gita it was the wrong number—the caller had wanted room 602 and his was 601. She stayed with him at the hotel almost every night until he left, and almost every night it happened. The calls were always in English and always in the form of a colloquial question or cliché. Once a man asked, "Is everything good to go?" and another time, "Is it always darkest before the dawn?" Each time he told Gita it was the wrong number, and she told him he should complain at the front desk, but he said it wouldn't do any good.

Of course, he had expected to be watched, but he hadn't planned on doing anything worth watching. He asked her once whether she was afraid that something would happen to her after he was gone, and she told him that the chairman of the Academy of Architects was a very close friend of her late husband, who had drowned himself in the Neva River three years ago. That was how she had gotten the position as the head and only librarian of the Academy of Architects. Still, he knew how precarious such connections could be and wondered whether the Academy of Architects itself was responsible for the phone calls. It was perhaps because of these concerns that, although he liked being alone with her in his room, he felt that their happiest times together were when they were not in the room—though he knew how much she enjoyed the privacy she had at the hotel, for she lived in one room with her two children and her mother in a communal apartment shared by four other families. On many evenings, he sat at his desk in the meager light reviewing his notes while she soaked in the bathtub.

They talked mostly about their children. Her son Shura, she told him, was quiet and was already proving to be quite a talented oboist. She hoped he might have a musical career. Her daughter, Vera, had little interest in music and books but was devoted to swimming. She practiced every day after school for hours, after which she came home and devoured huge amounts of food. In the photos she showed him, Isaac was surprised to see a boy who did not look small and thin although Vera was just as he had imagined—blonde and broad-shouldered and swimmerish. Gita was surprised that his girls did not take music lessons, and he explained that they liked music but preferred the written word to all other forms of artistic expression and that, though they did not seem to mind school, he worried sometimes that neither of them talked much about their classmates or their teachers. He told Gita that on Simone's last birthday he had suggested that she invite some of her classmates for a party, but she'd said that just wanted to have a quiet dinner, *en famille* (as they referred to such occasions), instead. He did not tell Gita, though he often thought about doing so, that his daughters were motherless and he wifeless. He knew that she assumed, because of his silence, that there was someone besides his daughters waiting for him to come home, but he could not tell her the truth, which was that being with her reminded him how much he missed Ulli. Instead he gave her all the gifts he had brought for his relatives, the snowsuits and pantyhose, the soap and aspirin. On their last evening together, Gita presented him with a photograph of Shura and Vera, standing stiffly in the park dressed up in their new snowsuits, and Isaac gave her the photo of Simone and Juliet, which he had brought to show his relatives.

Simone and Juliet tried to convince Katja Ladijinskaya that they all should take a taxi out to Kennedy Airport to surprise their father, but she said their father would not approve of such an extravagance, that the arrangement for the limousine had already been made.

"Let us bake him a welcome-home cake instead," Katja Ladijinskaya had suggested.

"Our father doesn't really like sweets," Juliet said.

"We will make plum tarts. Do you like plum tarts?"

Simone and Juliet did not answer because they had never tried plum tarts before.

Katja Ladijinskaya made a shopping list, and Simone and Juliet rode their bicycles downtown to buy the ingredients for the plum tarts. "Isn't it too cold to be riding bicycles?" Katja Ladijinskaya had asked them as they set off.

"We're used to it," Simone answered, though they had not ridden their bicycles all winter, and when they returned with the groceries, they could not unbend their fingers and their ears stung and they could not feel their feet. Katya Ladijinskaya made coffee to warm them up, though they would have preferred hot chocolate with cognac, which was what they always had with their father after shoveling snow.

For the first time since their weekend in New York, Katja Ladijinskaya seemed to have regained her passion for cooking. She had come home the night before with "four wonderful specimens" of sole for their father's homecoming meal, and by four o'clock the tarts were baked, the rice cooked, and the fish and the spinach ready to be sautéed in butter with a "splash of red vermouth and a dash of coriander." The three of them waited impatiently for the limousine, sitting in the living room in their good clothes. "You cannot greet your father in rags after such a long absence," she had said, and Simone and Juliet had not protested. Simone and Juliet took turns every few minutes jumping up and running to the window. "How can you concentrate on your books with that constant jumping up and down?" Katja Ladijinskaya asked, but she did not insist that they stay put. It began to snow heavily, and Simone and Juliet worried that their father's plane would crash or not be able to land. Katja Ladijinskaya chewed her fingernails, but they did not speak about the weather. The room grew dark so that it was difficult to read, but they did not turn on the lights, nor did they check their watches. Simone and Juliet grew hungry, but they did not ask about dinner. And then, just as Katja Ladijinskaya was about to say, "Well, I suppose we'd better turn on the lights," the limousine pulled into the driveway.

"I think I heard something," Juliet said.

"It's the wind," Katja Ladijinskaya said, but it wasn't the wind. It was their father.

After they had eaten dinner and had the plum tarts with their tea, Katja Ladijinskaya wanted to leave on the 8:36 bus.

"Don't be ridiculous," their father said. "Look at the weather."

"The buses are still running, and I'm sure you three want to catch up," Katja Ladijinskaya pointed out.

"There will be plenty of time for catching up," he said firmly. "In the morning we'll drive you. This is no night to be out on the road."

"What if it snows all night long?" Juliet almost asked, but she did not want Katja Ladijinskaya to feel that she wanted to get rid of her.

And so Katja Ladijinskaya stayed one more night, and it was not until the next day, after they had safely deposited her and the blue Samsonite suitcase in her apartment on 106th Street, that the three of them had a chance to catch up, though Simone and

Juliet responded to their father's questions with an unusual shyness, as if he were a teacher asking them particularly difficult questions. They kept their answers brief and simple: yes, they had fun with Katja Ladijinskaya; yes, Katja Ladijinskaya was a good cook; no, they did not go to the movies; yes, they spent one weekend in New York.

Their father showed them a photo of their cousins standing in the park wearing their new snowsuits. He did not show them photos of any of their other relatives because, he explained, they had been afraid to be caught on film, afraid that at some future date these documents of his visit would be used against them.

"Why weren't Vera and Shura afraid?" they asked.

"Because they are young and hopeful."

"And what about their parents? Weren't they worried?"

"We took it in secret," their father said in a whisper, as if the danger of the Soviet Union had followed him home.

carlito on pink

Instead of going out dancing with the others, Kenard decided he would stay home with Doña Beatriz and Carlito, take some pictures if they were up for it, which they surely would be, especially Carlito. He would be fine staying at the house with his host mother and brother. He would do some portraits and look through his latest photographs, give them titles. This is what he told the trip chaperones, and so they had gone off without him.

He has been taking a lot of pictures of Carlito, using the brightly colored walls of Doña Beatriz's house as a backdrop. He likes the texture of the walls, and how the colors change the way Carlito looks. Carlito on mint green is different from Carlito on pink or yellow. He looks almost sad on mint green, even though he is smiling like he always does. He is teaching Carlito, who is the same age as he is—sixteen—how to count to ten in English. He can remember up to three, sometimes even five, but then the next day they have to start all over again. Even in Spanish Carlito knows only up to seven, but Kenard is determined to teach him even though Carlito does not understand what numbers are. To him they are merely words that he is being asked to repeat, to remember. He has tried to get Carlito to understand that a hand has five fingers, that if you hold up all the fingers on one hand it is always five, that you don't have to count—*one, two, three, four, five*—but every time Kenard holds up five fingers, Carlito counts. He has taken a series of Carlito holding up fingers. Ten photographs. Ten numbers.

Doña Beatriz comes out best on pink. Her long, dark hair looks almost as if it were moving, blowing in the breeze perhaps, though in the living room, which is the room that is painted pink, there is not even the memory of a breeze. The whole house is like that, the hot air unmoving and relentless so that Kenard is always sweating, even when he lies still on the bed. Doña Beatriz and Carlito do not sweat, not even when they are eating, which is when it's the worst for Kenard; the sweat pours off his face and his eyes sting from the salt and his shirt sticks to his back. Doña Beatriz is worried that he is not eating enough, or at least that is what he thinks she is saying when she points to his food. He does not have the words to tell her that he has what the doctor called a delicate stomach, which means basically that the doctor had no explanation for his chronic stomach ailments, so he smiles and eats a few more mouthfuls, washing it down with Coca-Cola.

It turned out that Doña Beatriz's boyfriend would be having dinner with them. If Kenard had known that he was coming, he might have gone dancing with the others after all. Doña Beatriz's boyfriend speaks a little English because he worked in Miami for a few years when he was young. Kenard doesn't like him because he pats Carlito on the head as if he were a dog, ruffles his hair, and then ignores him. He doesn't like him because the first time he met him, he said that he could get Kenard a woman if he wanted one. "There are a lot of hungry women in Nicaragua," he said.

"No, thank you," Kenard replied as if the boyfriend had offered him another helping of food, and the boyfriend had shrugged and asked him whether he had a girlfriend.

"No," Kenard said. He hates that question and has learned that it is best to simply say *no*, to say it firmly, looking the person right in the eye so that they understand that that there is nothing to discuss, that *no* simply means *no*, that he has answered their question. Period.

Kenard also doesn't like him because Doña Beatriz acts the way his mother acts when she is trying to please a man. The whole time the boyfriend is there, Doña Beatriz has a permanent smile on her face and is constantly running off to the kitchen to get him more beer, and no matter what he is saying, her eyes are glued to him as if he were a movie. Kenard wants to tell Doña Beatriz that it isn't worth it, that in the end, the boyfriend will leave her no matter how quickly she jumps up to get him a beer, no matter how many special meals she makes. Worst of all, he will move from ignoring Carlito to becoming more and more impatient, angry even. When he was younger, some of his mother's boyfriends tried to be nice to him. They took him on excursions to places like the zoo and the boardwalk in Santa Cruz, but eventually they got tired of having a kid hanging around. Still, his mother's boyfriends could be a lot worse. Kenard knows this. He knows that there are boyfriends who beat women up, and the women's children, too. This is why he tolerates them even though he knows that in the end they will be unfaithful to his mother, that they will choose someone else over her and she will be left alone.

"I guess I'm just destined to be alone," she says when she finds herself without a man again, and he sits next to her on the couch and tells her that everything is going to be okay, that she is not alone because she has him, and she kisses him and tells him that she doesn't know what she would do without him. She makes him promise not to be a cheater and liar like all the men she has ever known. And he promises because he doesn't want to cheat and lie. He doesn't want to make anyone hurt the way his mother is hurting. Sometimes after the boyfriend disappears, she doesn't get out of bed for days, and Kenard brings her food and tries to get her to eat, and she eats just a little, just for him, because, she repeats over and over again, if she didn't have him, she would just kill herself. But then she snaps out of it, gets up and says that she was a fool to be crying over a man, and after a while there will be another boyfriend. His mother has no trouble finding a man. "It's much easier to find a man than to keep one," she says.

Kenard had not really wanted to go on this trip to Nicaragua, but his friend Ilisha had bamboozled him into signing up because she didn't want to go alone, though she wouldn't have been alone since altogether there were eleven of them. Ilisha was always talking about going far away from San Francisco and traveling all over the world, but Kenard liked staying close to home. He was particular about what he ate because of his stomach, and he liked to have his things around him—his music, his room, his computer. Plus, he was not good at Spanish. In fact, he hated Spanish class, couldn't roll his *r*'s, pronounced *pollo* "polo," didn't understand the grammar, had no idea, ever, what the teacher, who insisted on speaking only Spanish, was saying. He had passed the class only because he was polite and handed in all the homework, which he copied from Ilisha, who had, according to Ms. Silvestri, the Spanish teacher, a natural gift for languages.

But it was Ilisha who had backed out, thrown a fit as she often did, gotten tired of all the work they had to do to raise money—the car washes, the candy selling, the bake sales and silent auctions. The last straw for her had been the walk-a-thon. "What kind of fool would pay anyone money for walking?" she said after Ms. Silvestri had explained that walk-a-thons were a common way to raise money, that there were walk-a-thons for breast cancer and leukemia and Darfur, but she had refused to listen because she was, as she put it, "done with it."

Kenard does not know what it was that made him not stomp off after her. Perhaps he was tired of her outbursts. Perhaps he really wanted to go to Nicaragua after all and hadn't even realized it until then. Perhaps it was because, as usual, he felt bad for Ms. Silvestri, who worked so hard, much harder than any of their other teachers, and who had made a point of telling him that she hoped he would still be coming with them even though Ilisha was not, so Kenard had assured her that he was, that he was looking forward to it. "I am too," Ms. Silvestri said, longingly. "You will see that it is a different world, a completely different world."

He is fairly sure, however, that if he had not discovered the camera, he would not have stuck with the trip after Ilisha had given up. It was the camera's craving for new images that led him to wander farther and farther afield to neighborhoods that he had never even heard of, and sometimes his hunger for pictures was so great that he had to make rules for himself like someone on a diet counting calories, weighing the contents of each meal carefully, eating slowly, making the most of small portions. Had it not been for the camera, he would not have gotten the most pledges of everyone and encouraged all the others, who also were skeptical about the very principle of the walk-a-thon, to give it a chance. In the end, all of them had walked the full ten miles. That was the farthest he had ever walked before.

And now he is here, eating nothing but beans and rice—he hates beans, always has—and his stomach is in revolt, but he is used to that. He is even getting used to having to go outside to the bathroom and to throwing the toilet paper not into the toilet bowel but into the dirty yellow pail instead. At first he kept forgetting and he worried that the whole thing would back up just because of him, but now he reminds himself as he sits down on the toilet, "Don't forget about the paper, don't forget about the paper," and it has become almost second nature. He actually wonders whether he will forget and throw the paper into the wastebasket instead of the toilet bowl when he gets home. He wonders whether his father, who will be coming back to live with them after all these years, is the kind of father who gets mad at a son for throwing the toilet paper in the wastebasket instead of the toilet, where it belongs. He is learning, however, that even something as basic as where to put used toilet paper is not so clear-cut, not so black and white as it might seem.

His father is in jail for killing someone, but his mother has always claimed that he didn't do it, even though that didn't stop her from having her boyfriends. That is the way his life has always been—his father in jail, his mother with her boyfriends. "I can't just put my life on hold," she says. Then, just a few months ago, lawyers from the Innocence Project took on his father's case. Until his mother told him about the Innocence Project, Kenard believed that he believed in his father's innocence. Yet now, ever since her announcement, in his gut, right where it hurts when he eats something spicy, he can feel his doubt throbbing. Maybe, he thinks, it's easier to be taken in by a lie than by the truth, or maybe he had just been trying to fool himself all along. "They don't take up your case unless they're one hundred percent sure," his mother told him when she announced the news about the lawyers and the DNA that would prove it wasn't his father who had done it. But how can anyone be one hundred percent sure about anything?

Kenard wonders how long his father will stick around if and when he gets out, but he doesn't want to think about it too much. He doesn't want to think about whether he hopes his father stays or hopes he doesn't. He doesn't want to think about it because what is the point when he doesn't have all the facts, when everything depends on who his father is when he is no longer the man in jail, when he is beyond his exoneration.

After dinner, when the other students are at the dance, he wants to work on some self-portraits. He will set up the tripod. He wants to see whether he too looks sad on mint green or whether the combination of black and green will have a completely different effect and bring out the longing in his eyes, or the anger. He will call the photos "Kenard on Pink" and "Kenard on Yellow" and "Kenard on Mint Green." At home he has taken photographs of himself naked, lying on the floor and on the bed. He holds the camera up in the air as far away from his body as possible and shoots.

When he is out with the others, he shoots what they shoot—the cathedral and the lake, the colorful colonial houses. He snaps along with them as if he were just like them, and when he gets back to his room at Doña Beatriz's house, he deletes all the photos. These pictures seem dead to him. Maybe someday he will find a way to make objects come alive, but for now he wants to concentrate on portraits. Before he got interested in photography, he didn't give much thought to people. This did not mean, however, that he was rude. On the contrary, he always got up for the old lady on the bus and said "excuse me" and "thank you" and "please." "A polite and helpful boy," his fifth-grade teacher wrote on his evaluation, along with the usual negative comments like, "Kenard is often disengaged and unfocused and is, thus, not meeting his full potential." It was not until he started taking pictures that he really started paying attention to people. Once he began looking through the camera he noticed that there were others like him. There were other children who walked home by themselves with their hands in their pockets, not stopping to talk to strangers, not stopping to talk to anyone.

Now he sees people like him everywhere—on the bus especially. He wants to do a series of portraits of passengers. His idea is to take candid photos holding the camera at his stomach and nonchalantly pressing the button so that they don't even notice, and then starting a conversation, asking a question about how to get somewhere, sitting down next to them. He could get off with them and go wherever they are going. He likes the idea of going where they are going, knowing why they are going where they are going. Then he would show them the candid shot and ask if he could take some more pictures. He sees it as a book with the candid shots starting off each chapter. Maybe he could get someone to write short biographies of the people, or maybe it would be better without any words.

He writes down these ideas in the little notebook that Ms. Silvestri gave them to write down new vocabulary. The notebooks, which Ms. Silvestri had gotten from her mother's Spanish bookstore in New York, were from Bolivia, though they were just ordinary notebooks and didn't look at all like they were from another country. A lot of the other students threw theirs away or left them in the classroom, left them on the desk or lying on the floor, making it very clear to Ms. Silvestri that they could not care less about improving their vocabulary, but Kenard was not the kind of kid who did things like that. He appreciated the fact that Ms. Silvestri cared—cared, as she often told them, more about their futures than they did. In any case, he likes his little notebook, and he carries it with him everywhere. It is small enough to fit in his back pocket, which is what Ms. Silvestri told them when she handed them out. Sometimes in class if he has an idea for a photograph, he takes it out and writes in it, and Ms. Silvestri notices and smiles at him encouragingly, which makes him feel like he is lying.

They are all sitting in the living room watching television. The boyfriend's arm is tense around Doña Beatriz's shoulder, as if he is worried that she will escape. She smiles and says something to Carlito, who takes Kenard's hand and leads him into Kenard's bedroom, which, when Kenard is not there, is Carlito's room. "*Uno, dos, tres,*" Carlito says, holding up his fingers, and they practice counting for a while, in Spanish first and then in English. When Carlito gets tired of counting, they listen to music, sitting side by side on the bed, sharing the earphones. Carlito pulls Kenard up from the bed and they dance together, Kenard bent over so that he can be at Carlito's level and still share the earphones. He imagines what they must look like—Carlito making his moves, smiling, and Kenard trying to follow him so that they don't get disconnected from the music. Every once in a while the earphone jerks out of Carlito's ear and Kenard replaces it gently, holding on to Carlito's head.

Carlito takes him by the hand and tiptoes, finger over his mouth, "Shhhh," toward the living room. The boyfriend has his hand inside Doña Beatriz's shirt, and Doña Beatriz's mouth is slightly open. Their eyes are on the television. Kenard tries pulling lightly on Carlito's shirt to get him to go back to his room, but Carlito wants to watch. He puts his index finger on his lips again. "Shhh."

Kenard stands with him but he does not look, makes a point of not looking. Why don't they go into the bedroom? His mother and her boyfriends always go into the bedroom. When he was younger, he tried to imagine that it was his father in the bed with her on the other side of the wall, but when he was old enough to understand the details of what they were doing, he focused on not thinking about it at all. He put on his earphones and concentrated on the music.

"Come on," he says to Carlito, pulling him away from the doorway.

"*Cámara,*" Carlito whispers, holding his hands up to his face, clicking the air with his index finger.

"No," Kenard says, but Carlito leads Kenard back to the room and gets the camera. They return to the edge of the living room, tiptoeing quietly. They hide behind the doorway to the living room, peeking in and then hiding again. Kenard is afraid that Carlito will start laughing and Doña Beatriz and the boyfriend will look up and see them there. But Carlito is dead serious. *Click.* Another *click, click, click.*

"Enough," Kenard says, sure that they can hear the shutter clicking. He gently takes the camera from Carlito. "*Vámonos,*" he whispers, and they tiptoe back to the bedroom. Carlito wants to see the photos, so they sit down on the bed again and look at them, and Carlito points out the boyfriend's hand on his mother's breast and laughs. "It's not funny," Kenard says, but Carlito doesn't understand and keeps on laughing.

Doña Beatriz calls to them that it is time for dinner. The boyfriend is already sitting at the table, smoking a cigarette, waiting.

Doña Beatriz is in the kitchen and Kenard tries to go in to help her, but she tells him to sit down. She never lets him do anything, not wash the dishes, not even carry the dirty plates back to the kitchen. He sits at the table with the boyfriend and waits to be served.

If he could speak Spanish, he would tell her that he is used to helping out, that at home he is the one who washes the dishes, does the laundry, that he knows how to cook a few things. He has been fending for himself since he was ten, carrying the keys to the apartment (one for the entrance door and one for the apartment itself) around his neck on a leather cord. "Never take it off except for when you go to sleep at night," his mother had told him. "Never let anyone, not anyone, take it from you." When he first started wearing the cord, the leather smelled of Sunday shoes, but it has long since lost its odor. Here, though, the smell has returned, though it is not exactly as he remembers it. It is not an unpleasant odor, but it is not clean like the smell of new shoes. There is something more reminiscent of animals and sweat.

He thought he would leave the keys behind when he went to Nicaragua. They would be safe at home in the top drawer of his dresser, where he keeps them at night. But when he was all set to go, his suitcase waiting by the door, he felt for the keys as he always did every time he left the house, and they were not there, and he realized that he needed to have the keys with him, that otherwise he would always be reaching for them and they would not be there, and he would miss the weight of them around his neck and the way they clanked softly against each other when he walked. So just as the buzzer rang, announcing that the van was there to pick him up, he ran back for them.

When he was first entrusted with the keys, he took his new responsibility seriously and always went straight home from the Boys & Girls Club, where he went directly after school every day. There were plenty of opportunities for him not to do so. It would have been easy, for his mother did not return from work until nine at the earliest, but he was always happy to be home, to turn on the lights, get himself a glass of soda, turn on the television. Often he would fall asleep on the sofa watching television, and when his mother came home she would wake him. "Did you eat any dinner?" she would ask, and he always said that he had even if he hadn't because he did not want her to worry that he was not eating enough. Sometimes he would wake up in the night hungry, and then he would not be able to fall asleep until he ate something even though he didn't really want to eat, preferred just to sleep. He would get up quietly so as not to wake his mother, who did not sleep soundly. In the kitchen, he would stand at the counter with the refrigerator door open for light, eating whatever it was he found—bread and butter usually, or cookies.

Tonight's dinner is special because of the boyfriend. Doña Beatriz brings them each a bowl of soup and sets it in front of them. Kenard knows it is fish because he can smell it, could already smell it when he and Carlito were looking at the photographs in his room. He tried, as they looked at the camera, not to think about how he was going to make it through dinner. He hates fish. Inside each bowl is an entire fish, head and skin and eyes staring up at him, lying dead among a few bits of carrots and potatoes. Carlito is grinning, poking the fish in his bowl, loosening the flesh from the bone, lifting his spoon to his mouth.

Kenard begins with the potatoes. One by one, he extricates them from the broth, trying not to touch the fish with his spoon, though this, he discovers, is impossible. "*Muy bien*," he says to Doña Beatriz, who smiles. When he has finished the potatoes, he goes on to the carrots, and then he is left only with the fish. Doña Beatriz, the boyfriend and Carlito are all focused on the fish, making sure they get every piece of meat. The boyfriend lifts the head out of the bowl and is picking at the cheeks. *You can do it*, Kenard says to himself as the spoon touches flesh. He removes a small piece, pulls away the skin. It does not look so ominous when it is just that white flesh in the spoon. He puts it into his mouth and smiles at Doña Beatriz. He swallows. He does not allow himself to think of taste or smell. *Keep on smiling*, he says to himself.

The fish is now merely a skeleton of a fish and there is the gray skin that he managed to separate from the meat, floating in the broth. The fish looks like a child's drawing, completely distorted, its head much too large for its now spindly body, but there is something alive about it in its deadness, and he feels that if he hurries, he will be able to capture the last moment of the fish's life, the last memory. "*Cámara*," he says, and Carlito runs off to bring it.

He returns, holding it with two hands, carefully as if it were a baby. Kenard takes it, focuses in on his bowl, on what is left of his fish, *click*, and then the boyfriend's headless skeleton and the head, lying eyeless on the oilcloth. Carlito has eaten the eyes too, but not the cheeks. Doña Beatriz's fish looks like his—the head intact. He will call the photos "Carlito's Fish," "The Boyfriend's Fish," "Doña Beatriz's Fish," "My Fish." Of course Carlito wants to see the photos, which he finds so funny that he doesn't stop laughing until the boyfriend says something to him sharply, and he stops.

For dessert there is ice cream, and he and Carlito have two big helpings. He can feel the coldness of it making its way into his stomach. It feels soothing, this coolness, yet he knows the sensation for what it is—a prelude to a revolt on the part of his stomach, a sign of its rawness. He pictures his insides red and exposed, recoiling as they prepare for the next wave of food that is being imposed on them.

Doña Beatriz's boyfriend is telling a long story. Doña Beatriz stops him to ask him a question every once in a while, which seems to annoy him, and he answers her questions with the tone of someone who has been unnecessarily asked to repeat himself more than once. Kenard concentrates on the words, trying to pick out the familiar ones, but he can't recognize enough to even have an idea of what is being talked about. Carlito doesn't seem to understand either. He kicks Kenard under the table and Kenard kicks him back, and they both are trying really hard not to laugh. The story is coming to an end. Kenard can tell by the way the boyfriend's voice has slowed down and dipped that the story is taking a sad turn. Doña Beatriz reaches over and takes the boyfriend's hand, but after just a few moments he pulls his hand away and takes out a cigarette and lights it. Doña Beatriz keeps her hand right there, right next to where his hand had been. Then abruptly, in midsentence it seems to Kenard, the boyfriend stops talking, gets up and goes outside. Doña Beatriz stays at the table for a moment, smiles at Kenard, says something to him that he does not understand, and Kenard smiles back. She gets up and starts taking the dishes into the kitchen, and again Kenard tries to help, but she waves her hands in front of her face and says, "*No, no*," so he sits at the table politely until she has taken everything into the kitchen and he can hear that she has started washing up. Only then does he feel that he can go to his room.

Carlito follows him, of course. Kenard knew that he would, and though he would prefer to be alone, would like nothing better than to stretch out on the bed and listen to his iPod, he cannot close the door on Carlito, cannot wave his hands in front of his face and say "no" the way Doña Beatriz does when he tries to help. Carlito would just stand outside the door, waiting, and Kenard would sense that he was out there, just standing outside his door the way he does every morning with his arms held out stiffly at his sides so that there is a space between them and the rest of his body. Carlito wants to listen to music, so Kenard gives him the iPod, and Carlito hums along while Kenard records his photographs in the back of the notebook that Ms. Silvestri gave him. He keeps an accurate record of all his pictures, making sure to cross out the ones that he ends up deleting, the ones that do not make the final cut at the end of each day.

It seems that the boyfriend has come back inside. Kenard can hear him talking and Doña Beatriz laughing in that way that his mother laughs when she knows she is losing her man. It sounds now almost as if they were chasing each other around the house. Sometimes the laughter is closer, almost right outside the door, and then it fades away again. The boyfriend's voice ebbs and flows like when someone is messing with the volume of a radio. They are in the bedroom now. The walls are thin, thinner even than the walls in his apartment. He can hear them falling onto the bed, the headboard banging against the wall.

Carlito is dancing, dancing with his eyes closed, spinning slowly round and round, his arms spread out, his fingers stiff like twigs. Kenard takes out his camera and shoots, getting him from all angles but not moving himself, waiting for Carlito's body to turn, for his face to come into view. Carlito stops turning, lets his arms fall to his sides as if they are tired, as if he had been holding them up for a very long time, and rocks slowly back and forth, so slowly that the camera cannot capture the movement. In the bedroom next door the laughter is getting louder and louder and then it stops and is replaced by the sound of the headboard banging against the wall.

Carlito's mouth is slightly open, and Kenard gets closer to him. He wants to take a picture of his mouth, of his tongue. Kenard cannot tell whether Carlito senses him there, senses the camera at his face, but Carlito does not open his eyes and continues to move, slowly, slowly, and Kenard leans down and sets the camera gently on the floor, and as Carlito continues to dance, Kenard closes his eyes too, and with his fingers softly, slowly traces the outlines of Carlito's face—his lips, his cheeks, the eyes, the thinness of the eyebrows, again his lips, his tongue, slippery in his fingers like a frog. He likes the feel of Carlito's tongue escaping his grasp, of catching it and feeling it slip away, over and over again.

maximiliano

When Simone arrived at the airport in Asunción, she was met by a sullen taxi driver sent by her sister Juliet, who had not been able to get off early from her job teaching English to pick Simone up herself. The taxi driver insisted on carrying both of her bags, and she felt somewhat ridiculous walking behind him, bagless. He had to stop twice to catch his breath, but each time Simone offered to help he shook his head angrily. Simone suspected he had a heart condition of which he was not aware.

Simone was a home health care worker. She had begun working in this field part-time for an organization called Student Help for the Elderly when she was in college, and when she graduated, she was still working for Mrs. Levinson. Mrs. Levinson's son paid her well, above the going rate, since Simone was the only health care worker that his mother would tolerate. The job was meant to be a stopgap measure while she figured out what she was going to do with her life, so when Mrs. Levinson died two years later and Simone had still not figured out what her next step would be, she decided to go to Paraguay to visit her sister, for whom seeing the world was, at least for now, far more important than figuring out what she was going to do with her life.

Simone was surprised when the taxi driver pulled into a long driveway that led to a large, white Spanish colonial house. She supposed she had expected a hut or a garret, which was more Juliet's style. Simone knew that Juliet was living with a man named Raúl. Juliet had written to her about him. Simone imagined that this was his house. He had recently returned to Paraguay. He had been in what Juliet had termed *self-imposed exile* in Madrid for years but had returned for his father's funeral, and then he had not gone back into exile. His father had been a traveling salesman who had had children all over the country. Rumor had it that he even had one child with a Mennonite woman. According to Juliet, Raúl had not liked his father, and now that his father was dead, he had no reason to be far away from home.

The taxi driver brought her bags all the way to the front door, where he waited with her—though Simone had already given him a generous tip—until Juliet, who had just gotten back from work, answered the door. It had been only a year since Simone had seen her sister, but Simone's first thought was that she seemed thin, too thin. When they embraced, Juliet's arms felt brittle and limp. She looked as though she hadn't been outside in a long time. She looked, Simone thought, like a young version of one of her home health care clients.

Juliet led her from the foyer into a big living room that contained only one sofa and a few metal folding chairs. There were no decorations on the walls and no curtains on the windows. Juliet sat down on the sofa, so Simone sat on one of the folding chairs. They talked about Simone's trip, about how she had had to change planes three times, about their father. He was well. Juliet said that he wrote to her every week but that she did not write as regularly because she did not have much to report. "Paraguay is not very interesting," she said, a statement that Simone found odd because Juliet had once told her that she could not imagine a place in the world that was not interesting, that every place had its strangeness. For Juliet strangeness in itself was interesting.

A small, plump woman entered the room carrying a tray with two tall glasses of fresh grapefruit juice. They drank the juice, and Juliet told Simone that there were more grapefruits in Paraguay than anyone knew what to do with. "After it rains it smells of rotten grapefruit, and you always have to watch for fallen grapefruits when you're walking through the city." She paused before adding, "I have come to hate grapefruit juice."

"Then why are you drinking it?" Simone asked, and Juliet laughed, but she did not offer an explanation.

Without warning Juliet jumped up and grabbed Simone's bags. "Let me show you your room. You must be tired. Do you want to take a nap? Are you hungry? Do you want to take a bath?"

Juliet was not usually jumpy. On the contrary, she was the calm one, the one who was always telling Simone to relax, to play it by ear, but Simone was too tired to give her sister's behavior much thought. After all, they had not seen each other in a year. It would take some time for them to get into the rhythm of things with each other.

"Perhaps a shower will do me good. Maybe afterward we could go for a walk," she said. Once she was clean, she would be able to think about other things, she thought. Once she'd had a shower, they would be able to talk.

"Maybe," Juliet said. "Let's see how you feel."

Simone's room was large—as large as a classroom. In it there was a single bed and one metal folding chair. Again there were no curtains and nothing on the walls, which were painted a light mint green. "There's no closet," Juliet said, and Simone told her it didn't matter, that she could keep her things in her bags.

"Are you sure?"

"I'm sure," Simone said.

There was a bathroom down the hall with a big claw-foot bathtub and no showerhead. "Everyone here takes baths," Juliet said and laughed, though Simone did not know what was funny about this either. The bathroom smelled of mildew, and the bathtub was not filthy but definitely not clean. "Do you have some Ajax or something?" Simone asked.

"What for?"

"To clean the tub."

Juliet smiled as if Simone were asking her for something completely ridiculous, like a marionette or a shoehorn, but she went and got some Ajax. "Here," she said.

Simone scrubbed the tub and then took a long bath. The bath water smelled slightly of metal, like a bagful of pennies. She was not in the habit of taking baths and was certainly not the type to take long baths, but she was tired and wasn't yet ready for what was to come next.

When they were children, Juliet and Simone did not need to talk much. They could sit on the floor in one of their bedrooms and read or draw for hours without saying a word, but they liked the fact that the other one was present, sharing the air, thinking her own thoughts. Sometimes they would lie on their stomachs listening to records for an entire rainy afternoon. Now what Simone needed was a little more time alone. She let more hot water into the bath, sank down deeper into the water. Just a little more time and she would feel revived, ready to catch up, to make plans.

In her letter, Juliet had said that she was very interested in taking a trip up north to the Chaco to see the Mennonite communities and suggested that the three of them—she, Simone, and Raúl—could do that together when Simone came to visit. In her response, Simone had mentioned that she was also quite interested in seeing the Iguazú Falls, and Juliet had replied that everyone wanted to see the Iguazú Falls. "The Iguazú Falls are not what they are cracked up to be," she wrote. Simone figured she could go on her own if Juliet did not want to accompany her. Simone did not mention that she would prefer to make the journey to the Chaco without Raúl, but that is what she thought, though of course she had not even met him yet, and it was possible that she would like him very much and that the three of them would have a great time together driving up north to see the Mennonites.

When Simone came downstairs after her bath, Juliet was not there. She found the small plump woman in the kitchen peeling potatoes. "Juliet?" she asked.

The woman said something that she did not understand.

"*Gracias*," Simone said. She explored the house. There were four more bedrooms upstairs, two of which were completely empty. The bedroom that she assumed was Juliet and Raul's was furnished like hers, only their bed was a double and in the far corner of the room was an old armoire with a mirror built into the doors. Of course, she did not enter the room. She always respected people's privacy. In her line of work that was very important. There were many live-in health care workers who snooped around—rifled through the drawers of their frail charges, read their letters, looked through photo albums, stole—but not Simone.

She sat on the sofa in the living room and waited for Juliet to return. The bath had made her even more tired, so she lay down on the sofa and closed her eyes. When she woke up, it was getting dark. She could hear the sounds of something frying coming from the kitchen, and a radio was on somewhere in the house. "Juliet," she called from the couch. "Juliet."

The small plump woman came into the living room, wiping her hands on her skirt. She said something and Simone thanked her again, and she went back to the kitchen. Simone got up and turned on the light, thinking that Juliet might have left her a note. She sat down on the couch and began crying quietly so the woman in the kitchen would not hear her, though it might have been comforting to have the woman come in, speak some words, sit down next to her. Crying was not something she did often, and she felt that she should get up from the sofa, take a walk, a run even, but she could not rouse herself. Eventually, she dozed off, jerking awake every so often only to drop off again. Finally, after what seemed like a long time but turned out to have been only an hour, she was awakened by the sound of a child singing.

"This is Maximiliano, Raúl's son," Juliet said. She and a boy of about six who was dressed in a school uniform—navy blue shorts and a white shirt and navy blue blazer—were standing very close to her in front of the couch. They were holding hands.

"Hello, Maximiliano," Simone said. "You have a beautiful name."

"He doesn't speak English," Juliet said, and then she translated what Simone had said into Spanish.

He smiled and said "*gracias*" and something else, which she did not understand. Juliet translated. "He says that it's not a name for a small child."

"But some day you will be grown up," Simone said.

"That is a long time from now," he said sadly.

"It is not as long as you think," Simone said. "Before you know it, you will be a man."

"Like my father," Maximiliano said.

"Yes, like your father," Simone said.

"But I will be different from my father," Maximiliano said.

"Of course you will be different, but you will be grown up like him," Simone said.

"And his mother?" Simone asked, turning to Juliet.

"His mother's Spanish," Juliet said. "She couldn't stand living here, so she went back to Madrid. The agreement is that Maximiliano will spend the summers in Spain. But she hardly makes an effort to call him, so it's not like she's dying to see him. Raúl's plan is to do nothing when summertime comes, to wait and see whether she'll ask for him or just let it go."

"Maybe it's not that she doesn't want to see him. Maybe she's just feeling guilty because she left," Simone said.

Juliet shrugged. "Maybe."

"You didn't tell me there was a child," Simone said.

"There's nothing to tell. He's very good, like we were when we were children. He's my very patient Spanish teacher. He gives me lists of words to memorize and tests me on them every morning at breakfast. He reads a lot and draws birds. Do you want to see the drawings?"

"Sure," Simone said. Juliet spoke to Maximiliano, and he ran out of the living room and up the stairs, returning with a large album, which he set down on the sofa next to Simone. Then he ran off to get another one. He repeated this process until there was a pile of five albums on the sofa. He sat down next to her and showed her each drawing, pointing out various features. He did not seem to mind that she did not really understand what he was saying. The drawings were almost perfect. They looked like faded photographs but were, in fact, color pencil drawings done with a light and steady hand.

After they finished looking at the drawings, the three of them ate avocado omelets and boiled potatoes. Again they drank tall glasses of grapefruit juice. When they finished eating, Maximiliano excused himself and Juliet and Simone drank coffee. Simone drank two cups even though she was in the habit of drinking coffee only in the morning.

"I could use a walk after all that caffeine," Simone suggested.

"How about a run instead? We could cover more ground."

"A run would be even better," Simone said. "Have you been running a lot?"

"Not really. How about you?"

"You know me. I always run," Simone said. "I would lose my mind if I didn't."

As soon as they were outside, Simone felt stronger. "It's perfect running weather," she said, and they were off.

They had to keep their eyes focused on the ground so as not to slip on the squashed grapefruit that lay like decapitated heads all along the sidewalks. Juliet and Simone didn't believe in chatting while running, so they didn't talk much. Juliet pointed out the important sites—the cathedral, the museum, the port. It was obvious that she hadn't been running much lately, but Simone didn't say anything. She just kept a slow, steady pace. When she noticed Juliet was getting tired, Simone said that she was worn out from the long plane ride, so they headed back. Then Simone took another bath in the water that smelled of metal, and when she came downstairs again, Raúl was there.

He was not what Simone had expected. He was old, not as old as their father, but in his forties. And he was blond. He looked German because his ancestors were, in fact, German. "There is nothing German about our family anymore, however, since we have lived in Paraguay for four generations," Raúl said.

Raúl spoke perfectly correct British English with only the slightest accent, pronouncing all his letters carefully. He used a lot of words rooted in Latin such as *ascend* and *perpetual*. "Raúl speaks many languages," Juliet explained. "Spanish, of course, German, Guaraní, the indigenous language of the Paraguayan Indians, and Latin and Greek, of course. He studied with the Jesuits and can actually carry on a conversation in Latin. He's like a priest," she said, laughing, and Raúl smiled.

"So how do you find our little country?" Raúl asked Simone.

"I have not been here long enough to have many impressions," Simone answered carefully.

He smiled, uncrossed his legs, and then immediately crossed them again.

Maximiliano came downstairs with one of his sketchbooks and sat on the floor at his father's side. He waited until there was a break in the conversation and then he asked his father if he wanted to see his latest drawings. Raúl took a long time looking at each one. He asked his son questions and his son answered. To Simone he said, "My son only wants to draw birds."

"He is still very young," she said.

"Yes, but there is something unnatural about his obsession. He has no interest in any other animals. My brother has a farm, and Maximiliano completely ignores the other animals when we visit them. He walks around the property looking up at the trees. Just last week we saw a family of monkeys and he cried and cried, enraged that his beloved birds had to share their trees with such horrible beasts."

Simone appreciated Maximiliano's loyalty to birds, but she did not know how to explain this to Raúl. He did not seem like someone who had respect for things like devotion and loyalty. "I would like to see monkeys," Simone said instead.

"Tomorrow I will take you to my brother's farm to see monkeys," he said, standing up. "And now, if you'll excuse me, I have work to do." He walked over to Juliet, kissed her lightly on the forehead, tousled Maximiliano's hair, and nodded to Simone. Then he was gone.

They ate another light meal—more avocados, a bland soup with yucca, carrots, and a few pieces of beef. Juliet and Simone drank a bottle of Argentinean wine, and Maximiliano taught Simone how to say everything that was on the table in Spanish—*plato, tenedor, cuchillo, cuchara, vaso, servilleta*. He made her repeat the words until she pronounced them just right. When she had learned them all to his satisfaction, he wanted to take her outside to learn the names of trees and flowers and birds, but Juliet said it was too dark outside.

Simone slept for a long time, and when she woke up the next morning, Juliet was just about to leave for work. "Make yourself at home," she said. She, Raúl, and Maximiliano would be back in the early afternoon. "We're taking you to Raul's brother's farm," she said. Simone had brought *The Collected Poems of Wallace Stevens* with her and took the book down to the living room. She read her favorite poems, poems that she had read hundreds, perhaps thousands, of times before, poems that she knew by heart. She read them aloud, very softly because she knew she was not alone—she could hear the woman working in the kitchen. The woman brought her a glass of the ubiquitous grapefruit juice.

"*Café?*" the woman asked and Simone said, "*Sí, gracias,*" and after a while the woman brought her coffee and a plate of bland cookies. "Avocado?" Simone said, holding her hands together in the shape of an avocado, but the woman smiled at her the way someone smiles when they don't understand a joke and returned to the kitchen, coming back after a few minutes with another glass of grapefruit juice. She thanked the woman, and the woman smiled and waited until Simone lifted the glass to her lips.

Simone was starving by the time Juliet, Raúl, and Maximiliano returned, but the farm, it turned out, was on the other side of the country, near the Brazilian border, so there was no time for lunch. As it was, they would not arrive before nightfall. Simone figured they would stop along the way, but they only stopped at a gas station, where she bought some nuts, which she shared with Maximiliano in the backseat. He ate the nuts one at a time, slowly, closing his eyes and chewing carefully.

They did not arrive at the farm until after ten, and once they made the turn onto the property, they drove for another twenty minutes before they arrived at the house. "All this is his property," Juliet explained. "You'll see how beautiful it is in the morning—jungle all around us."

There was a guard with a semiautomatic rifle at the gate. He saluted and pressed a button, and the gate opened. In front of them the house was completely lit up as if there were going to be a party. In the driveway they were met by a team of young men dressed like tennis players, in white shorts and shirts. The young men took their bags and led them to the house, where Raúl's brother stood in the doorway, smiling, rubbing his back against the doorjamb. Juliet had explained in the car that he suffered from some kind of skin ailment that made his back itch. When he was sitting, he squirmed in his chair like a child at a piano recital, and when he stood, he stayed near the walls, rubbing against them like a cat. He spoke the same correct and not quite accentless English that Raúl spoke. "Welcome to my home," he said to Simone, stepping away from the doorway to shake her hand.

He led them to the living room, which was decorated in a modern style—chrome and leather and glass, black and white. Raúl's brother's wife, who was Brazilian and much younger than he, was waiting for them, sitting at the edge of a white leather sofa. She was dressed for a discotheque—high-heeled silver mules, a short skirt. She got up to greet them as they entered the room, moving toward them as if she were about to break into dance.

Once they were all seated, a young maid wearing a completely white dress, so that she looked more like a nurse than a maid, brought them scotch. Raúl's brother explained that scotch was cheaper in Paraguay than in Scotland because Paraguay was a duty-free zone. He told Simone that he would be happy to get her whatever she wanted—cognac, cigarettes, whiskey. She thanked him for his offer but explained that she liked to travel light, that she did not want to be weighed down by bottles and such things. His smile seemed to imply that he knew she was making a big mistake that she would later regret.

Raúl and his brother left the room, taking Maximiliano with them. Juliet and Raúl's brother's wife chatted. Simone could tell that Juliet was trying hard to think of things to say and that the wife was answering but wasn't really trying to keep the conversation rolling. The wife kept staring at Simone. When Simone finished her scotch, the wife poured her another one without asking whether she wanted more.

The wife addressed a question to Simone, and Juliet translated. "Do you have children?"

"No," Simone said.

The wife smiled and said something to Juliet, and because Juliet did not translate it, Simone decided that she was not obligated to participate in the conversation any longer, so she got up to go outside.

"Where are you going?" Juliet asked.

"Outside," Simone said. She could tell that Juliet wanted to come with her. "Why don't you come too?"

"You go," Juliet said. "I'm fine here."

Outside Simone could hear the sound of millions of insects, and it reminded her of being in a snowstorm. Eventually she discerned other sounds besides the insects—men's voices, leaves rustling. Something was scrambling around in the bushes. It smelled of meat cooking, of barbecue.

"What are you doing outside by yourself?" Raúl said, startling her, but she didn't jump or flinch. Maximiliano was riding on his shoulders. He was looking straight ahead, sitting up straight, stiffly, and Simone could tell that he was not enjoying himself up there, that he would have preferred to be on the ground.

"Nothing," she said though it was obvious that she was just standing there, that she was not engaged in any activity.

"Well, we'll be eating soon," Raúl said. It was almost midnight.

They stood around a little longer without speaking, and then they all went back inside. Raul lifted Maximiliano down from his shoulders. The boy's legs were shaking.

An entire side of barbecued beef, including the intestines, liver, kidneys and heart, had been prepared for them. They ate the meat with thick slices of bread and drank six bottles of wine between the five of them. Maximiliano ate scrambled eggs with tomato sauce and was taken to bed by one of the maids immediately after finishing his dinner. Simone excused herself soon afterward and was shown to her room by the same maid who had attended to Maximiliano.

Over Simone's bed was a painting of the Virgin Mary with her heart exposed. The painting was cracked and the colors muted with age. The Virgin's eyes were without expression, like glass eyes, and her mouth was too small and slightly pouty, like that of a thirteen-year-old girl forced to spend the evening with adults. Her hands were flaccid and boneless, the fingers too thin. Simone tried to read but the words floated around the page, so she turned off the light and concentrated on listening to the insects, trying to distinguish individual insect voices from the general cacophony of the night. Every once in a while a human voice interrupted her concentration, but soon she could not distinguish human from insect and she fell asleep.

The next day Simone awoke at six. She thought of waking Juliet, but she did not know how long Juliet had stayed up the night before, so she took a bath and read from a biography of Graham Greene until Juliet came downstairs. As it turned out, Raúl and his brother and his brother's wife had gone back to Asunción shortly after Simone had retired. Simone asked Juliet what was so important that made it necessary for them to drive such a long distance after a heavy dinner with so much wine, and Juliet said it was something to do with the business.

"What do you think of Raúl?" Juliet asked.

Simone did not know what to say because she did not like him, though she could not put her finger on exactly why.

"I like Maximiliano," Simone answered.

"So do I," Juliet said. "He's very smart."

"Yes, that's obvious," Simone said.

They ate breakfast, more avocados and grapefruit juice and eggs. Maximiliano, who had been delivered to the breakfast table by one of the maids, told them about a girl in his class who cried every time she heard the word *flower*, so the teacher had banned the word from the classroom, though she herself had forgotten on a few occasions. "It seems that if you know you can't say a word you find it popping up all over the place," Maximiliano said. "All the storybooks use it."

"Why does she cry when she hears *flower*?" Juliet asked.

"I don't know. She just does," he said, and then he whispered the word very quietly twice, "*Flor, flor*," as if to test them, to see whether they might cry also.

It was decided that after breakfast the three of them would take a bird-watching walk. Maximiliano had his own binoculars, which he wore proudly around his neck, but he was careful to make sure that both Juliet and Simone got a chance to use them every time they spotted a new bird. He was good at being quiet so as not to scare away the birds. When Juliet or Simone tried to talk, he turned around, put his index finger to his lips, and opened his eyes really wide. After they had been walking for about half an hour, he spotted a toucan high up. He pointed and looked through his binoculars for what seemed like a very long time. Then he handed Simone the binoculars so she could take a look. When everyone had had a turn, Maximiliano called to the toucan, cupping his small hands around his mouth so his voice would travel. "Be careful, toucan," he said, and the toucan flew away.

They came to a broad mango tree, thick and squat and wide like a tree in a Gustav Klimt painting. Maximiliano wanted to climb it, so Simone and Juliet lifted him up to the lowest branch, from where he scrambled into the thick of the tree so that they could no longer see him. They heard him laughing and talking as if he were sitting in a café, chatting with a friend. Because it had rained the night before, there was no dry place to sit down, so Simone and Juliet stood in the sun, waiting.

"How did he get so interested in birds?" Simone asked.

"I don't know. He just likes them."

"If I had a child, I would like him to be like Maximiliano," Simone said.

Before Juliet could answer, they heard a shrill cackle and a flapping of leaves coming from the tree. "Maximiliano," Juliet called, but he did not answer. There was more scurrying, and they saw Maximiliano about ten feet above them, scooting out onto a branch. Squatting on the same branch, leaning jauntily against the trunk of the tree and watching Maximiliano, was a monkey. Maximiliano stopped, gripped the branch tightly, and turned to look at the monkey. He did not speak or cry but held the monkey's gaze. Juliet and Simone approached the tree slowly, and Maximiliano lifted one hand from the branch and put his index finger to his lips the way he had done before when he was worried about frightening the birds, so they just stood there directly underneath him, holding up their arms, ready to catch him if he fell.

The monkey edged toward Maximiliano, then stopped. Maximiliano clenched his hands more tightly on the branch. It was obvious that the monkey was thinking about what to do next. Should he leap on the boy, push him to the ground? Should he scratch out his eyes or bite? Simone could sense that something terrible was going to happen, that the monkey just could not figure out the form that his torture would take.

"Jump!" Simone screamed. Whether he understood the word or just intuitively understood what she was telling him to do, she did not know, but Maximiliano jumped. Simone did not catch him, but she broke his fall, hitting the ground first with him on top of her.

Except for a few minor scratches, Maximiliano was unscathed, but Juliet did not see it that way. "How could you tell him to jump?" she screamed.

"The monkey would have scratched out his eyes or bitten off his hand. Do you know how deadly a monkey bite is? It's like a human bite."

"It was just sitting there! It wasn't doing anything!"

"But it was planning something. Couldn't you feel it?"

"You're crazy!" Juliet said. She scooped him up and walked as fast as she could, back toward the house.

"Wait a minute," Simone said, running after her.

Juliet started running also, though it was no effort for Simone to keep up with her. "The monkey would have scratched out his eyes," she said again.

"How do you know?" Juliet said, still running, Maximiliano's feet banging against her thighs.

"I just know."

"How could you just know what a monkey is thinking?" she said, and Simone let her run ahead and into the house, up the stairs to the bathroom, where she and Maximiliano stayed for a long time. Finally, Juliet came back downstairs. She told Simone that she had cleaned Maximiliano's wounds and put him to bed. "He's very tired," she said.

"Is he sleeping?"

"Yes. Let's not tell Raúl about this."

"If you think that's best. But what about Maximiliano? Won't he tell his father?"

"No, he won't say a word," she said, and Simone knew it was true.

"What if he asks about the scrapes?" Simone asked.

"I'll just say he fell," Juliet said.

Maximiliano slept until late in the afternoon, and when he woke up the three of them ate ice cream, and because it was raining, they sat on the living room floor and played checkers. None of them mentioned the monkey.

By dinnertime Raúl, his brother, and his brother's wife still had not returned, so they ate the remnants of the previous night's barbecue and retired to their rooms. Simone stayed up late listening to the rain and reading the biography of Graham Greene. She had bought it especially for the trip and found it engrossing, even though she had never thought much of his novels, despite the fact that she had read every one of them. She thought that if she could learn to like his books, she would feel the urge to travel, to have adventures in foreign lands. She was not sure why she believed this was something she should do, but she did. Perhaps it was because she and Juliet had spent so much of their childhood dreaming of adventures. Perhaps it was because such things were so important to Juliet.

At some point late in the night, Raúl and his brother and his brother's wife came home. Simone heard them climb the stairs. She heard their laughter coming from down the hallway. Then it was silent again, except for the rain.

The next morning Simone awoke before sunrise and went for a run. She ran down the long, curveless road that connected the farm to the main highway. It was hard running because the road was still muddy from last night's rain. Her calves ached for the last few miles from too much gripping and securing, and by the time she reached the house, she could not feel her feet. They were like weights shackled to her legs, holding her down. Her legs and arms and clothes were covered with orange mud.

When she walked in the door, Maximiliano ran to meet her. He said something, and everyone except Raúl laughed.

"He said that you look like a painter, like a painter who only likes one color," Juliet explained. Then she added, "Where have you been?"

It turned out that Raúl had planned an excursion for the day.

He was taking them to Iguazú Falls, and they had all been ready and waiting for over an hour. Simone apologized profusely even though she had not been informed about the excursion beforehand.

"It's too late to go now," Raúl said. It was only 8:30.

Juliet took Raúl aside and they talked in whispers. Juliet put her hand on his shoulder and he moved away. After a while, she took his hand and he did not pull away, though he still did not move closer to her. Simone stood there with orange clay all over her, and Maximiliano sat on the floor looking overly intently at his drawings. There were more whispers and a smile or two on Juliet's part. Finally, Raúl returned to where Simone was standing. "Well, if we hurry, there's still time," he said.

On the way to the falls, Simone sat in the back with Maximiliano. Raúl had come back in a different car, a big, silver Mercedes. It smelled of leather and cigarette smoke, and every time Simone opened her window, he would close it with one quick flick of a button. Maximiliano paid no attention to any of them. He sat with his nose pressed against the window looking out. Simone wondered what it was that made him so calm. She wondered whether it was from watching birds.

They came to the park and walked down the path that led to the falls. There were butterflies everywhere, thousands of them, hovering overhead, as if they were about to descend upon them, suffocate them with their colorful, dusty bodies.

Raúl was proud of the butterflies. "I bet you've never seen so many butterflies before," he said.

"No," Simone answered. "They're kind of frightening."

"Frightening?"

"You don't find them scary, unpredictable?"

"How could anyone be afraid of butterflies?" Raúl asked, looking to Juliet for help.

Juliet just shrugged.

Maximiliano was walking ahead of them. He wasn't skipping or running excitedly the way children do in parks. Rather, he was walking slowly, looking down as if he were trying to keep the butterflies at bay by pretending he did not even notice they were there. Still, they swarmed around his face, and some settled on his shoulders and his back. Simone wondered whether he could feel them, or whether their weight was too insignificant for him to notice. The adults followed Maximiliano through the cloud of butterflies, but the butterflies did not land on any of them though Simone could feel them brushing against her arms and legs.

They came to an open space and there was the falls—a giant wound of gushing red water. Simone had not expected the falls to be red. She had pictured something cooler—white water over rock. Raúl swooped down on Maximiliano, who was bending over to pick up a rock. He lifted his son high in the air and set him down on his shoulders and took off in a full gallop toward the edge of the cliff. Maximiliano did not hold on to his father's head or neck the way children do when they are riding on shoulders. He sat straight, like a knight, gripping with his knees. They reached the railing and looked out over the falls. Simone was sure that Maximiliano had his eyes closed. After a while Raúl turned, and he and Maximiliano waved.

Simone asked Juliet if Maximiliano had been to the falls before. She remembered how Juliet had dismissed the falls as a tourist destination in her last letter.

"We drive here almost every weekend," Juliet said. "Raúl likes the falls. Sometimes we stand at the railing for two hours just watching."

Simone wanted to bring up the letter, but instead she said, "It's like when we used to go to Weehawken to see the view of New York." It wasn't really like that at all since their father didn't take them there every weekend. They only went with guests, and they never stayed for more than ten minutes, though it often seemed much longer than that because no one wanted to be the first person to say he wanted to go.

Juliet laughed. "This is more impressive, don't you think?"

"Only because it's not familiar. I bet Maximiliano would prefer Weehawken," Simone said.

"Maybe, but he doesn't have much interest in large things."

"No, he doesn't," Simone said.

When they got back to the farm, they ate the usual supper of eggs and avocados and drank too much wine. Simone became unusually talkative, telling stories about Mrs. Levinson, about how she kept all her valuables in the refrigerator so she would always be able to find them. Both Raúl and Juliet laughed too hard at the stories, and Maximiliano sat listening carefully. He did not laugh when his father and Juliet laughed, the way someone who was trying to pretend he understood would do, and Simone felt that he understood what she was saying, even though she knew he couldn't. When the maid came in to take him up to bed, he left reluctantly. At the top of the stairs, he turned around and waved.

Soon after Maximiliano went to bed, Simone retired also, though she knew she would not be able to sleep until the wine wore off. She tried to read the Graham Greene biography, but she was too tipsy to concentrate. After a while, she heard Raúl and Juliet talking and laughing as they ascended the stairs. "Shh," Raúl said. "Don't wake the children."

Simone still could not sleep. After the house had been quiet for some time, she heard a door open. She got out of bed and opened her own door quietly. She saw Maximiliano creeping down the hallway toward his father and Juliet's room. She thought perhaps he was sleepwalking, so she followed him but at a distance. When he reached his father's door, he turned the knob, opening the door just enough to slip in. Simone approached the door, but she did not enter the room. From the doorway, she could see Raúl and Juliet naked, lying on the bed facing each other asleep, the sheets in an unruly pile at the foot of the bed. Maximiliano stood close to his father, his back to the doorway.

For several minutes Maximiliano watched his father sleep, and then he lifted his hand, holding it up in the air over his father's head. He held it there for a moment, but then he lowered it again without touching him, and Simone did not know whether Maximiliano had been about to strike his father, to hurt him so that he would wake up startled and afraid, or whether he had only meant to rest his hand on his father's head for a moment, just long enough to feel his warmth, and then leave him to his dreams.

sonya's mood

Whenever Sonya Cohen is in one of her moods, she puts on the scratchy old 78s from Bolivia. They sound right to her, even though they are full of static and skips. Her son, Ezra, bought her an eight-record set called *Music from the Andes*, but the sound is too clean, too perfect. That is not the way she remembers it. She lights a cigarette, takes a sip of gin and tonic, closes her eyes, and lets the music envelop her.

Recently Ezra has been talking about taking her back to Bolivia for her sixtieth birthday. He can afford it; that is not the problem. He has a good job in advertising. But she doesn't really want to see how the small town of Rurrenabaque has changed.

She was eleven when they escaped from Vienna to Bolivia, and by the time they left Bolivia to come to New York, she hardly remembered the gray buildings of Vienna or the interminable holiday dinners in their apartment in the center of the city, a city that had once been, according to her mother, the center of the world. She had not known *that* Vienna. She had known the gray, cold winters, and the uncomfortable school clothes, and the hours and hours of penmanship homework. She had known her sullen uncles, who wore frayed black suits and mumbled prayers on the holidays—prayers that no one bothered to explain to her, prayers in a language that no one ever thought of teaching her. And by the time they left Rurrenabaque six years later, all that was gone—the tattered Hebrew texts, the uncles.

Luis had cried when she'd told him they were going to New York. She had never seen a man cry before. When they said goodbye to all their aunts and uncles and to her grandparents and friends in Vienna, not one man had cried. But Luis had cried, and she would never forget him. *He is probably dead by now*, she thinks. They all died so young there. No, she would not want to return now. It would not be the same. Better to just sit in the fading light and listen to the records. Dan, her husband, has called to say that he won't be home until eight, so she has plenty of time for the records, plenty of time for the gin.

Dan had thought that her moods would improve once he finally agreed to move to the city. She'd petitioned him about it for years, ever since Ezra had gone away to college, but it had taken Dan eight more years to give in. He had loved their big colonial house in Connecticut, liked barbeques and mowing the lawn. He needed someplace to relax after a full day's work in the city. He needed to get away from the noise and drugs and crime. He worked hard; he had ulcers.

In Connecticut Dan had tried in vain to encourage Sonya to play tennis at the country club and take classes at the community college. For a while she'd had a job at a boutique that sold overpriced Italian clothes, but it made her feel even more useless to work just to keep herself busy. She preferred to read, to walk. She wrote letters to her two children—Ezra, who lived in the city, and Ester in Albuquerque. Once a month, she went in to the city. She went to a matinee, took a walk, met Ezra for dinner at a Chinese restaurant. Dan tried to get her to go in more often, but she hated feeling like a tourist, in for the day then back to the suburbs. She didn't want to *visit* the city. She wanted to live there. She wanted to live in an apartment with a river view and go out in the morning to buy the *New York Times* at the newsstand on the corner.

Her moods got so bad that in the end, Dan really had no choice. That last year in Connecticut, he would often come home to find her still in bed with a half-empty bottle of gin on the night table, the ashtray overflowing. So he gave in. They sold the six-bedroom house and bought a two-bedroom apartment on West End Avenue. It took them a while to find the right place, a place with a river view—$300,000 for a two-bedroom apartment with a kitchen that needed remodeling. Dan almost cried, but he had no choice. They could not go on the way they had been.

The first year in New York it was as if they were newly married. They went to the opera, to the theater, to museums. They ate out almost every night. But they both got tired of so much activity, and after a while, they slipped back into old habits. Dan worked late; he came home; he was tired; he ate dinner; he read books on military history and astronomy; he went to sleep. And Sonya's moods returned. Still, it was better than Connecticut. She could spend entire days just walking. She lingered in the Village, drank espressos on Bleeker Street, wandered through Chinatown and Brooklyn Heights. Sometimes she took the ferry to Staten Island and back. Sometimes she headed off into the Lower East Side, which had changed so much since the days when she and her mother used to buy cheap clothes from the Jewish peddlers on Delancey Street.

The last 78 has finished playing, but Sonya does not get up to lift the needle off the record. She thinks maybe they could go to a movie when Dan comes home. They could go out and grab something to eat. It is Friday night after all, and Dan doesn't have to work tomorrow. But he will be tired. He is always tired. He will want to stay home and read the latest book on the Crimean War or whatever war it happens to be.

When she married Dan thirty years ago, he had no hobbies. He liked to dance; he liked to eat. They used to go to jazz clubs in Harlem. In those days, that's what all the City College students did. She has not been to Harlem since then. Maybe, she thinks, I can take a walk through Harlem one of these days. I bet it has changed so much since we used to go there. Tomorrow morning, perhaps, she will walk up Amsterdam to 125th Street. Then she will head east, past the Apollo Theater. How dangerous can it be in the daytime on a Saturday?, she thinks.

She feels better now, revived because her Saturday is planned. She will not have to sit around and wait for Dan to muster the energy to go to a movie or out for lunch. She gets up and lifts the needle from the record. It is time to take a shower, put on something cool, make a salad, prepare the fish for dinner.

By Saturday morning Sonya Cohen has lost her desire to go to Harlem. First of all, it is too hot. Already at eight o'clock, steam is rising from the sidewalks, and the buildings on the other side of the street dance in a glimmering heat haze. Anyway, Rick has called and invited her to brunch. And she can't refuse Rick. It certainly would be much more pleasant to have brunch in the Village with Rick. The only unpleasant part is that she will have to tell Dan. Dan doesn't like Rick. He doesn't like that she and Rick go to French movies together. He doesn't like that they go to overpriced restaurants, where, he says, the portions are so small you walk out hungry. But what can Dan really object to? She suspects that what Dan really doesn't like is that Rick is homosexual. Of course, she doesn't ask him about it because he would deny it. In any case, she needs to have her own friends.

Sonya hopes that brunch with Rick will help expel the malaise she hasn't been able to shake all week. Last night she had one of her cat nightmares, so despite the promise of a pleasant day, she is out of sorts. She has had cat nightmares ever since they came to New York over forty years ago. The dreams started in the apartment in the Bronx, where she lived with her parents until she married Dan. The Bronx was filled with cats. They crawled around the alleys at night and darted into her path when she returned home from a friend's house or one of the Puerto Rican dances she used to go to, especially in the beginning, before she mastered English. The dreams are always the same. She is in a room and the door is closed, but the crack under the door is large enough to let the cats in. She tries stuffing the gap with towels, but the cats eat through them and push their way into the room—dozens upon dozens of cats—and they jump on her, claw at her face, rip her to pieces.

She should be used to the dreams by now, should be able to ignore them or laugh at them, but they always shake her up. Brunch with Rick is one of the few things that she can imagine might make her feel better. Lunch with Ezra would be even better, but she seldom sees him these days. He's so busy. He calls her every week, and they talk for an hour, the way they used to talk, but he works so much now, just like his father. He rarely leaves work before eight, and the weekends are for his girlfriend. Sonya likes Ezra's girlfriend. She's a bit shy, but smart. She's getting her PhD in art history at Columbia. They will probably get married soon, but Sonya is in no hurry. It will have to happen someday, she supposes. It happens to most people. Unless you're like Rick, of course. He doesn't have to worry about getting married.

It was Cynthia, Ezra's girlfriend, who introduced Sonya to Rick. They had been friends at Brown—he was a graduate student when she was an undergraduate—but he had dropped out; he couldn't imagine getting a teaching position in someplace like Oklahoma and being stuck there the rest of his life. So when his father died and he inherited some money, he opened up an antique store in the Village. He has a good eye and loves to talk to people. He can talk for hours about a nineteenth-century Italian bowl. In fact, he's made himself a nice little fortune selling antiques. And he gets to travel a lot. He is always trying to get Sonya to go with him to France or Spain or Indonesia. He loves Indonesia and he is sure that she would love Indonesia too. "It's like Bolivia," he says, but she doesn't think so.

Sonya plays the Bolivian records again all morning. She can tell they are getting on Dan's nerves, but she knows he won't say anything because he understands that the slightest thing can send her over the edge. Dan understands her moods better than anyone. Ezra is always trying to do something, to help, to listen, but Dan has learned that the best thing to do is nothing, to wait it out, let her listen to the old records, let her drink too much gin and have brunch with Rick.

Now Sonya is in a tizzy about what to wear. If it weren't so hot, she could wear the lilac scarf that Ezra brought her from California. She looks good in scarves because of her long neck, and the lilac suits her black hair and pale skin. Rick says she looks more Castilian than Jewish, but then Rick is in love with Spain. He lived there for two years after college and had a passionate affair with a Flamenco guitarist. At first Sonya didn't believe him about the guitarist, but he showed her pictures of the two of them together: a small, dark man in a red silk scarf and Rick, tall and blond with startling blue eyes. Rick had grown tired of his Flamenco guitarist, so he came home, but he still loves to talk about him, especially about his hands. The thought of the guitarist's hands can bring tears to Rick's eyes. Sometimes when they have had too much to drink, Rick asks Sonya to tell him about Luis, and she does. Then they cry together about Luis and the Flamenco guitarist.

When Ezra was a child, he used to cry so much, so much more

than Ester, who would get angry if her mother tried to help her button her coat or tie her shoes. "I can do it myself," she would scream, and she'd stomp off to a corner but would never cry. Once Ezra had found a wounded bird in the snow on the way home from school, and he had lain down next to it to keep it warm. He'd stayed with the bird until his fingers and toes were numb from the cold, leaving only when the bird was dead. When he got home, he cried and cried, and Sonya cried too. They both cried until they fell asleep.

Sonya Cohen gives her hair one last fluffing up as she climbs the stairs to Rick's third-floor apartment in a well-maintained brownstone on Morton Street. She rings the doorbell, and Rick opens the door. He smells of expensive soap, Spanish perhaps, and the apartment smells of coffee.

"Sonya, Sonya, you can't imagine the state I'm in, like a schoolboy really. It's ridiculous. I'm making an omelet, spinach and Gruyère. I hope you're not watching your cholesterol—everyone is watching their cholesterol these days, except me, of course. Isn't it beastly hot?" He whisks her into his large, sunny kitchen, puts her in a chair, lights her cigarette, brings her a glass of wine.

"Yes," she says, "it's very hot. I almost fainted on the subway. I should have taken the bus, but it takes so long."

"I hope you didn't want to go out, but I've been up since six fretting, so I thought I'd keep myself busy by making something here. It's cooler anyway."

"I'd rather stay in, too. I don't feel like dealing with crowds and waiting on line. So what is it?" Sonya asks, leaning forward in her chair, ready for Rick's story.

"Nothing, really. It's so silly. Let's eat first. How are you, Sonya? You look beautiful. How is Danny Boy?"

She wishes he wouldn't call Dan that, but she lets it go. She always lets it go because that is just the way Rick is. He's like that with everyone. "Dan's fine. He's still working too much. We might go to Israel in September. He's always wanted to go, and I suppose I'd like to go just once."

"You could go via Greece. Greece is wonderful in the fall."

"I don't know whether we'd have the time. Dan can't, or says he can't, take more than two weeks off."

"I think it'll be time for me to make a trip in the fall too." Rick flips the omelet. "Perfect. I hate to break an omelet. Well, I guess we're ready," he says, swooping down on Sonya's wine glass and refilling it. He grabs the bread basket, the butter, and the pan with the perfectly flipped omelet. Sonya knows not to help him. He is much more efficient than Sonya, who is always forgetting something, running back to the kitchen for the salt or the bread. But she has never really liked cooking. Not that she's a bad cook, but cooking, like most practical tasks, makes her nervous.

"Actually, it all seems so silly when I think about it, but I just had to tell someone, so I guess I'm stuck now," Rick says when they are settled at the table.

"I'm listening," Sonya says. "Mmm, did you use sage in the omelet?"

"Yes, just a tad. It's not too strong?"

"No, it's perfect."

"Well, that's a relief," Rick says. "Sonya, it's really so absurd. I think I'm in love. There, I've said it. I haven't felt like this in ages. It's so time-consuming. I can't sleep; my stomach is a wreck. I don't even know whether I can eat this," he says, pushing his food around the plate with disgust.

"Well, who is it?"

"It's someone I met through Arthur. You know, my accountant. He's always trying to set me up with someone, but this time I was caught off guard. Arthur and Bruce had one of their dinner parties, and that's where we met. He's not even that attractive. He is, but he isn't. He's a little heavy, not fat, but he doesn't exercise, and he smokes. And he's very interesting." He leans back, out of breath almost from having gotten it off his chest.

"What's his name? Where's he from? What does he do?" Sonya asks.

"He's from Indiana. Can you believe it? I don't even know if I've ever met someone from Indiana before. He's young, twenty-four, and has only been in New York for three months. He works for *Harper's Magazine* and is very political, very serious. Can you believe it? But I can't stop thinking about him."

"Have you seen him since the dinner party?"

"Oh, yes, that's the problem. We've seen each other four times this week. We've been to the movies, that horrible film *Field of Dreams*. I don't know why we saw it. We both hated it. We both hate baseball. We should have walked out, but we sat through the whole thing. I've called him at work, just to say hello. It's absurd."

"Why is it absurd? If you like him."

"Because I don't know what's going on. We haven't even touched each other, if you can believe it."

"What's so strange about that? You hardly know him." Sonya is perfectly aware of Rick's sexual habits. Once, he told her, he had eight sexual encounters in one day. One of them was in the bathroom at the Metropolitan Museum. "I'm glad you're being more careful," she adds. She worries about AIDS. She worries more than Rick does, or more than he says he does.

"It's weird because it's like dating. I don't even know what dating is, but I think that's what we're doing."

"Maybe you should talk to him, ask him what he wants," Sonya suggests.

"I can't talk to him. I mean, I can, but not about that. I'm just afraid to make a move. I feel like a teenager, like the time I was in love with Tony Rossi, and we used to spend hours and hours in his basement playing ping pong, and all I could think about was that I wanted to touch him, but I could never bring myself to do it."

"He is gay, isn't he?" Sonya asks.

"Of course he's gay. Ah, Sonya, you don't understand. Things used to be so simple and now everyone's afraid. But it's not AIDS that we're afraid of, not really, but it's AIDS that made such a mess of everything, forced us to stop and examine what we were doing, which no one really wants to do, examine, that is, not if they can help it. I know I'm not making sense. You know what I did this morning after I went shopping? I went to the pier. It was already so hot. The Hudson was like a steam bath. I walked out onto the pier, all the way to the end, and waited, and sure enough, some guy came up to me and gave me a blowjob. You can always count on the pier. Afterward I felt much calmer. I still feel better, so much better—really."

"I don't see what that has to do with—" she pauses. "You didn't even tell me his name."

"Philip. His name is Philip."

"I don't see what that has to do with Philip."

"Nothing, Sonya dear, nothing. I'm just not used to feeling like this."

"So how did it help you?"

"How did what help me?"

"Going to the pier," Sonya says, looking away.

"It just did. You should try it. It brings you back to the world, away from dreaming. Dreaming can be so destructive."

"Why didn't you just call Philip up? Why didn't you call him and invite him to brunch instead of me?"

"Because I couldn't. It's not done."

"What's not done?"

"Oh, stop baiting me, Sonya. You wouldn't do it. You wouldn't call him. You wouldn't do anything."

"What do you mean, I wouldn't do anything?" she says.

"You just wouldn't. You'd lock yourself up in the apartment. You'd make dinner for Danny Boy. You'd go to goddamned Israel."

"What's wrong with going to Israel?"

"There's nothing wrong with going to Israel," Rick says softly, composing himself. "Sonya, don't you like the omelet? You're not eating."

"I am eating," she says, and she begins to eat deliberately, one forkful right after the other.

"Sonya, darling, I didn't mean to upset you. It's just that I'm in a state. You understand, don't you?"

"Of course I understand. Can you pour me some more wine, please? I'm so thirsty. It must be the heat."

They talk about other things—about Rick's business, about a new shipment of Persian rugs that is selling like hotcakes. They talk about Ezra. "If Ezra were free, I'd go after him. He's sweet," Rick says.

"You wouldn't," Sonya says, and they both laugh.

Before they know it, it's five o'clock, time for Sonya to go. "Dan and I are going to try that new Indian restaurant on Columbus, though I don't think I'll be able to eat much. I'm still stuffed."

When Sonya Cohen emerges from the subway at 86th Street, she is not ready to go home, and she wonders why she left Rick's place so early, why she said that about the Indian restaurant. She stops to look in a shoe store. She tries on a pair of sandals, but they make her feet look bloated. She thanks the saleswoman and goes back out into the thick summer air.

I could use a drink, something refreshing, she thinks as she passes Marvin Gardens. She has never really noticed the place before, and she certainly isn't the type to have a drink by herself at a bar. If she goes out for lunch, she'll have a glass of wine, but that is at a table, not at a bar. She turns around and walks back to

Marvin Gardens and goes in. The air-conditioning hits her hard like wind coming off the Hudson in the winter, she thinks. She takes a seat at the bar. She orders a gin. What am I doing at a place like this with all these people Ezra's age?, she thinks. But she is here. She has ordered. She lights a cigarette.

After she has had three drinks, she begins to notice a young man who is watching her from the other end of the bar. She smiles at him. He is handsome, dark, Arab-looking, well dressed. She likes people to be well dressed. The man gets up. Sonya follows him down the stairs to where the bathrooms are. She watches him go into the men's room. She follows him inside.

"Oh hi," he says as if he is not at all surprised to see her there.

"Hi," she replies.

When she is done, he zips up his pants and strolls out of the bathroom without saying a word, not even thank you. She stays there, kneeling on the floor, gagging. She leans over the toilet bowl and tries to vomit, but she can't. After a while she gets up and goes to the sink. She washes her face, rinses her mouth, fixes her hair. She thinks that it was good she decided not to wear the lilac scarf Ezra had given her.

She leaves Marvin Gardens without looking at anyone, without looking to see whether he is still at the bar. She walks home, concentrating on not thinking about anything, hoping that Dan will not be there.

She is lucky. There is no one home. The apartment is hot, but she doesn't turn the air-conditioning on. She goes to the bathroom and peels off her clothes. She runs the shower really hot so that it burns. She stays in the shower a long time, and then she dries herself slowly and applies moisturizing cream to her stomach, her legs, her shoulders, her breasts. She puts on her summer robe and goes to the living room. She stacks the 78s high, as high as they go. She turns on the stereo, and the first record drops into place. Slowly she walks to her chair by the window and lets herself sink into it. She closes her eyes. She does not want to see the view, does not want to see the Hudson River or the rooftops and water towers or clouds or sky. All she wants is to let the music touch her softly, like rain, like love.

chinese opera

The Buchovskys were at the Chinese opera the night Danny McSwene was murdered. The three of them—Simone, her sister Juliet, and their father—had been there all day, from nine in the morning, to be precise, and were not released from the performance until ten that night. The coroner's report said that he had died somewhere between eight and midnight, so his death might not have occurred during the performance but, rather, when they were eating dinner later. The exact time was not crucial. Still, Simone would always think of the actors' endless wailing and excruciatingly slow movements and their white, painted faces whenever she thought of Danny McSwene's last moments.

Their father had a long tradition of dragging them to such events. When they were small Simone was sure he searched carefully for the most tedious and difficult performances to bring them to. She thought he was trying to teach them something—patience perhaps, or tolerance—but now that she was twelve, her older self realized that he simply had had no idea what torture these outings were for young children, and she was convinced that he thought she and Juliet enjoyed them as much as he did. He liked to refer to the three of them as a trio. Simone always imagined them as a trio of flute, violin, and piano, though she could not say who was which instrument, but as she got older she could not think why her imagination had settled on such shrill and plucky instruments. They were really much more like bassoons and violas—unassuming and hardworking.

It was especially cold the day they went to see the Chinese Opera, the day that Danny McSwene died, and it was cold in the theater too. Simone kept her coat and gloves on the whole time. She imagined, however, that the actors were warm enough. They were heavily clad, and their movements, as slow as they were, seemed to require a lot of effort—each placement of the foot, each slow swoop of the hand, even the eyes labored, prowling slowly, meeting the gaze of the enemy or a lover. At first she enjoyed the performance. She liked the feel of the gong reverberating in her legs and in her heart and was amused by the costumes and the stories, the details of which were outlined in the program. She fell into a sort of trance, concentrating on color, sound, and movement without thinking about the plot or the cacophony, but after the one intermission, during which the three of them ate black bread with butter and honey that their father had prepared at home, she grew increasingly bored.

Their father had promised to take them to their favorite diner after the performance for a late dinner. Their father was able to get them to do just about anything—sit through a lecture about the diary of a foot soldier in Napoleon's army or the uncut version of a movie about the Russian icon painter Andrei Rublev—if he promised that they would have dinner at a diner afterward. Though each had their favorite form of eggs, all three of them always ordered eggs. Eggs and milkshakes.

During the second half of the opera, it had grown even colder, and all Simone could think about was that she was cold, though she never would have dreamed of excusing herself, of asking permission to take a walk or go to the Coliseum Bookstore, which was just a stone's throw away from Lincoln Center, where the marathon Chinese opera festival was being held. So she sat through the rest of the performance, rubbing her hands and dreaming of the oily warmth of the diner. Later, after hearing the awful news about Danny McSwene, Simone felt that she should have been using this time more wisely instead of wasting it, thinking about the cold and wondering whether she should order a mushroom or cheese omelet.

Danny McSwene was their favorite of their neighbors' seven sons. There was quite a difference in age between the oldest sons, who were twins and lived together in South America, where they worked for a philanthropic organization, and the youngest, who had graduated from high school the year before. Danny was right in the middle and the quietest of all the McSwene boys, although Simone did not really know the twins or Alan, who was next in line and had been shot in the lung in Vietnam and then married a Japanese woman he had met when he was on leave. When Alan came home, he and his wife lived with the McSwenes until they could get settled. It was summer, and Simone remembered them lying on lounge chairs in the backyard for hours at a time until they both were very brown. With the two youngest boys, Simone and Juliet played catch, but though both girls were athletically inclined, they were no match for the McSwene boys who included the two of them in their games nonetheless, perhaps, Simone thought, because they secretly longed for sisters.

But what they really looked forward to were the nights when Danny McSwene babysat. As soon as their father was out the door, the excitement would begin. The first step was to clear the living room, move everything—the couch, the chairs, tables, rugs—through the kitchen and into the family room. They did this efficiently and carefully, making sure not to scrape the walls or scuff the wooden floors.

"You don't know how lucky you are to have wooden floors," Danny McSwene said every time. "Carpeting is the scourge of the modern world. How on earth is anyone supposed to dance on carpeting?"

When all the living room furniture was piled into the family room, they changed into their dance clothes. Danny McSwene wore special shoes and wonderful black pants with pleats. He had a collection of silk shirts—pink and purple and green. Simone and Juliet put on their good school shoes. One night Simone got to wear pants and lead while Juliet wore a dress and followed and the next time they switched roles.

Danny McSwene had a collection of records that he carried in a green, patent leather satchel he had bought in New York specifically for that purpose. They always started with waltzes and ended with the cha-cha, their favorite. His favorite was the tango, which Simone found a little embarrassing, especially when he insisted on more passion. "Where's the passion?" he would call over the music. "More passion, more passion!"

At the end of the dance sessions, they had always put the furniture back exactly right, so their father wouldn't notice, though he would not have minded, would have been happy to know that they were having such a good time with Danny McSwene. Still, Danny had made them promise not to tell anyone, and they never did, not even after he was dead.

They did not learn about Danny's death until two days after it happened because they were not in the McSwenes' inner circle. Though they were all fond of one another and happy to be neighbors, the Buchovskys kept their distance as good neighbors do, and the McSwenes kept theirs. And so they learned about his death from the local newspaper, the *Suburbanite*. On the front page there was a photo of Danny McSwene in his chef's uniform. He had just graduated from the Culinary Institute of America the spring before and had moved to New York, where he had gotten a job at a restaurant with stars. The newspaper said that he had been found in his apartment in Greenwich Village—shot in the back of the head. *Execution style*, they called it.

They did not go to the funeral. Their father avoided religious ceremonies of any kind, even weddings, and tried to have as little as possible to do with all things religious, though they sometimes went to concerts at Riverside Church in New York because he was a great admirer of liturgical music, especially Russian Orthodox, which he played at full volume while they cleaned the house every Sunday morning. Despite his appreciation for religious music, it was a matter of principle with him to fight against what he called the *forces of unreason* in his own, quiet way, as he did when he was drafted into the army and refused to declare a religion on the official paperwork. Even when the superior officer explained that they needed a religion so that they would know how to dispose of his body if he died, their father was unbending.

"You can just leave me there for the vultures, like the Zoroastrians do," her father had said. Every time he told the story, Simone could not help but imagine her father dead, the vultures pecking at his flesh, his eyes, and when he came to that part she always laughed so as not to let on that she was frightened.

"Like who?" the officer had said.

"The Zoroastrians," her father had answered.

"Is that a religion?"

"Yes," her father had said. "They leave their dead exposed to the elements and the vultures in what they call the tower of silence."

"How do you spell that?" the officer had asked.

Her father had spelled it out for him.

The man had grabbed the form, crossed out *none*, and written *Zoroastrian*. "There, now you have a religion. Now you can die."

Still, even though Simone was afraid to see it, she felt they should be there to watch Danny McSwene's body be let down into the earth, to throw a clump of dirt onto the coffin as she had seen mourners do in movies. "Don't you think we should go?" she asked her father just an hour before the funeral was to begin.

"It's much more important to pay our respects afterward," he explained. "They won't even notice who's at the church."

"But for Danny," Simone said.

"Do you think he was a believer?" he asked.

"I don't know. We never talked about it," Simone said.

"Well, if he wasn't, he would have preferred us not to go," he said.

"But we don't know whether he was or wasn't," she argued.

"No, we don't," he said, leaving her with nothing to argue against, for one cannot argue with incertitude.

"What if it were a Zoroastrian funeral?" Simone asked. "Would we go then?"

"Maybe," he said. "At least then it would be all out in the open."

"What would be out in the open?" she asked.

"Everything," he said. "Everything we don't want to see."

"Like the wound?" she asked.

"Like the wound," he replied, taking her in his arms, for she had begun to cry.

When they saw the mourners arriving back at the McSwenes' house after the funeral, Simone, Juliet, and their father went over to pay their respects. They dressed all in black. The girls wore Danskin tops and had made a special visit to the Tenafly Department Store to buy black skirts and tights. Their father wore his funeral suit. They brought a bottle of vodka and baklava because their father said they should bring something not too elaborate. At the McSwenes' house, there were plenty of black scarves and black ties and black shoes, but they were the only ones all in black. They stood awkwardly in front of the picture window that looked out onto the McSwenes' backyard where, just the summer before, Simone and Juliet had played catch and flipped baseball cards.

Their father made his way around the room, shaking hands with Mr. McSwene and all the remaining McSwene boys. When he had finished conveying his condolences to the men of the family, he joined his daughters at the window. "Mrs. McSwene is upstairs in the bedroom," he said. "I think you should go see her."

They climbed the stairs to the second floor slowly. They had never been upstairs before. The McSwene boys had been outdoor companions, and it never would have occurred to them to visit their rooms, look through their books, listen to their records. Mrs. McSwene, all in black also, was lying on top of a cream-colored bedspread like a giant felled chess piece. Surrounding her, on both sides of the bed, were women of all ages, the two oldest seated near her head holding her hands and the younger women closer to Mrs. McSwene's feet, kneeling on the floor, clasping her legs.

No one noticed Simone and Juliet as they stood in the doorway watching. Simone wanted to flee, but she knew they could not simply turn around, descend the stairs, and tell their father that they had not known how to approach Mrs. McSwene. He would not have understood about the barrier of women. And they could not have lied and said they had spoken to her when they hadn't. It would have made them sad to lie to their father about such a thing. Juliet pulled on the sleeve of Simone's black shirt, but Simone ignored it. She was focused on Mrs. McSwene's grief. She moved toward Mrs. McSwene and, as if she were Moses and the women the Dead Sea, they parted before her.

"I would like to extend my condolences," she said, but all Mrs. McSwene did was tilt her head without looking in her direction, as if she were blind and trying to hear more clearly. "Of all your boys, Danny was my favorite," Simone said, and Mrs. McSwene began to weep. She twitched on the bed and gasped, and the women ran back to hold her hands and wipe her brow. Someone brought a glass of water, and the older women pulled the weeping Mrs. McSwene up on her pillows and held it to her lips, and when she would not drink, they tried pouring it into her mouth, but the water ran down her chin and onto her black dress.

"She doesn't want to drink anything," Simone said quietly, and all the women turned and stared at her. Juliet ran out of the room.

"Come closer, Simone," Mrs. McSwene demanded in her raspy, smoker's voice that was raspier still from crying. "Sit down."

Simone sat down and closed her eyes. Mrs. McSwene pulled her closer and whispered directly into her ear, "He was my favorite too." Then she turned away and started to weep again.

When Simone returned to the living room, the mourners were looking out the picture window, watching the bright pink winter sun setting. They were standing, holding their drinks as if poised, waiting for that last burst of pink to disappear so that darkness could fall. Her father was not one of the sunset watchers. He was leaning against the wall looking at a large art book, which he was holding up with one hand.

"Simone," he said as if he had been worried that she was lost.

"It's getting dark," Simone said.

"I suppose we should be going. Where's Juliet?"

"I don't know," Simone said.

"We must find her, then," her father said. He returned his book to the shelf. The sun had set and the mourners had dispersed from the window and formed small clusters around the living room, talking quietly, more quietly, it seemed, because it was dark. Someone turned on the overhead light and everyone looked up, as if they had been caught in a searchlight. A woman began weeping. "Should I turn it off?" the man who had switched it on asked.

"No, it's getting dark," someone answered for all of them.

They walked silently back home. Their father wanted to make scrambled eggs for dinner, but no one was hungry, so they had chamomile tea and zwieback, which is what they ate when they were sick. That night Simone could not sleep. She tried reading, forcing herself to read what she called the *pretty poems*, the ones she usually skipped over—Wordsworth and Cummings, Houseman. She hoped, for some not-very-well-thought-out reason, that flowers and love and small hands would cheer her up, but she could not rid herself of the image of Danny McSwene sitting at his desk with a bullet hole in the back of his head. She tried to imagine what kind of person would feel compelled to *execute* Danny McSwene, who had always been so polite and had a dimple in his left cheek.

Simone closed her eyes and pretended she was sleeping in a house overlooking the ocean. The house was humble—a small, whitewashed cottage with a fireplace and stone floors. She tried listening for the crashing of the surf on rocks and the sound the wind makes on water. But Danny McSwene entered her cottage by the sea, sat in her simple wooden chair in her simple kitchen with cast-iron pans and earthenware pitchers. He sat down and said that he was very, very tired and asked for a glass of water. "Please," he said, and blood was pouring out of his head and onto his shirt, and a puddle of blood formed on the stone floor at his feet.

Simone got up then, walked quietly down the stairs, put on her coat and gloves and scarf. She stood in the backyard looking at the back of the McSwenes' house. She had expected it to be dark, but to her surprise, the house was totally illuminated, and she could see clearly into the empty living room and kitchen. She saw the furniture and the bookshelves and the fireplace.

She walked toward the house, and when she reached it, she stood in the flower bed underneath the living room picture window, her breath clouding the glass. She stood there waiting for someone to come down the stairs, but no one appeared, so she stayed put, stood there in the dark and cold until dawn. She wanted, then, to turn around and walk back to her warm house, get under the covers, sleep finally, but she remembered Danny and how he could feel neither heat nor cold, nor long for sleep, so she stayed.

Finally, just when dawn was turning to day, she saw Mrs. McSwene descending the stairs, pausing on each step as if to make sure it was strong enough to take her weight.

Mrs. McSwene stepped off the last step and walked into the living room. She paused in the middle of the room. Her lips were moving, and then they stopped, as if waiting for a reply. Mrs. McSwene was wearing a robe, and Simone imagined the women helping Mrs. McSwene change out of her black funeral dress. She wondered whether she would have preferred to keep it on. Something seemed to startle Mrs. McSwene, and she swung around, and before Simone could drop to the ground or run, Mrs. Mc-

Swene saw her. Because Simone did not know what else to do, she waved. Mrs. McSwene walked to the window and pressed her face to it, and her faced seemed like some separate thing trying to push its way through the glass.

Finally, Mrs. McSwene opened the back door and Simone entered. "Sit," Mrs. McSwene said, pointing to the sofa, and Simone sat down. Immediately, Simone began shaking. "How long have you been standing out in the cold?" Mrs. McSwene asked.

"A long time," Simone said.

"I'll bring some whiskey," Mrs. McSwene said and walked over to the liquor cabinet. She carried two very full glasses of whiskey back to the sofa and sat down next to Simone. Her robe had come undone, and Simone could see Mrs. McSwene's thighs, so she averted her eyes. Mrs. McSwene noticed that her thighs were exposed and stood up to adjust her robe, then sat down again, farther away from Simone. She reached into her pocket for a pack of Newports, tipped a cigarette out, and lit it, inhaling deeply. Simone took a sip of whiskey.

"I need your help," Mrs. McSwene said.

Simone leaned in toward Mrs. McSwene.

"I want you to tell them to go away," Mrs. McSwene said.

"Tell whom to go away?" Simone asked.

"All of them—my sons and sisters and the cousins and friends and in-laws. I don't even know who they all are, but they seem to know me, know that what I need to do is eat soup and rest and cry. They keep telling me that I should cry, that crying will do me good."

"But, I . . ." Simone's hands began to tremble, so she put them under her thighs, and pressed down hard upon them. "But I don't know them," she said.

"What?" Mrs. McSwene asked.

"I don't know them," Simone repeated.

"Of course, you can't tell them," Mrs. McSwene agreed. "You're just a child." She pulled out another cigarette and held it gently in the palm of her hand as if it were a baby bird.

"I didn't say I couldn't tell them," Simone said. She thought of Danny and how he would have known how to get them all out of the house without making anyone feel bad.

"So you'll do it?" Mrs. McSwene took her hand.

"Yes," Simone said. "Where are they?"

"They're everywhere. You'll just have to start opening up doors," she said.

Simone climbed the stairs slowly, thinking that the only thing she wanted now was a plate of her father's heavy, hot kasha, thinking that if she ate enough of it, she could finally fall asleep, sleep way into the afternoon until it was dark. She sat down on the stairs and tried to muster the courage to open the doors to the rooms where the sleeping mourners lay. She knew that Danny would have wanted her to help his mother, who had loved him more than she had loved her other six children. But Simone couldn't do it. Back down the stairs she went, softly, so as not to make the floorboards creak. She turned the latch and opened the front door and stepped outside where the sun was now bright and ricocheted off the remaining patches of snow, catching her right in the eye as if she were the killer.

In the days that followed, Simone avoided the McSwenes' house, so she did not know whether the flock of cars that stood in their driveway had thinned slowly or whether they had all disappeared at once like geese from a lake. Once they were all gone, she wondered whether Mrs. McSwene missed having them all there, trying to get her to eat and drink and cry and bathe. She imagined Mrs. McSwene lying on the living room couch and Mr. McSwene standing in front of the fireplace playing the bagpipe that always stood in the corner near the sofa. But maybe he stopped playing the bagpipe after Danny's death. Maybe all they wanted was quiet, but this is something she would never know.

The Buchovskys did not talk to the McSwenes much after Danny's death. They waved from their side of the fence and left them bags of apples from their apple tree on their back porch.

But sometimes at night before she fell asleep, Simone would imagine herself finding Danny McSwene's killer, cornering him in a dark alley, smashing his head against the wall while he begged for mercy and leaving him there, bleeding on the street. It was always raining in her presleep fantasies, and in the distance she could hear cymbals crashing like at the Chinese opera, and she moved in rhythm with them until they ceased completely and all she could hear was Danny's executioner calling out for her help: "Don't leave me here, don't leave me. Have some mercy, for God's sake, have mercy."

THE FLANNERY O'CONNOR
AWARD FOR SHORT FICTION

David Walton, *Evening Out*
Leigh Allison Wilson, *From the Bottom Up*
Sandra Thompson, *Close-Ups*
Susan Neville, *The Invention of Flight*
Mary Hood, *How Far She Went*
François Camoin, *Why Men Are Afraid of Women*
Molly Giles, *Rough Translations*
Daniel Curley, *Living with Snakes*
Peter Meinke, *The Piano Tuner*
Tony Ardizzone, *The Evening News*
Salvatore La Puma, *The Boys of Bensonhurst*
Melissa Pritchard, *Spirit Seizures*
Philip F. Deaver, *Silent Retreats*
Gail Galloway Adams, *The Purchase of Order*
Carole L. Glickfeld, *Useful Gifts*
Antonya Nelson, *The Expendables*
Nancy Zafris, *The People I Know*
Debra Monroe, *The Source of Trouble*
Robert H. Abel, *Ghost Traps*
T. M. McNally, *Low Flying Aircraft*
Alfred DePew, *The Melancholy of Departure*
Dennis Hathaway, *The Consequences of Desire*
Rita Ciresi, *Mother Rocket*
Dianne Nelson, *A Brief History of Male Nudes in America*
Christopher McIlroy, *All My Relations*
Alyce Miller, *The Nature of Longing*
Carol Lee Lorenzo, *Nervous Dancer*
C. M. Mayo, *Sky over El Nido*
Wendy Brenner, *Large Animals in Everyday Life*
Paul Rawlins, *No Lie Like Love*
Harvey Grossinger, *The Quarry*
Ha Jin, *Under the Red Flag*
Andy Plattner, *Winter Money*
Frank Soos, *Unified Field Theory*
Mary Clyde, *Survival Rates*
Hester Kaplan, *The Edge of Marriage*

Darrell Spencer, *CAUTION Men in Trees*
Robert Anderson, *Ice Age*
Bill Roorbach, *Big Bend*
Dana Johnson, *Break Any Woman Down*
Gina Ochsner, *The Necessary Grace to Fall*
Kellie Wells, *Compression Scars*
Eric Shade, *Eyesores*
Catherine Brady, *Curled in the Bed of Love*
Ed Allen, *Ate It Anyway*
Gary Fincke, *Sorry I Worried You*
Barbara Sutton, *The Send-Away Girl*
David Crouse, *Copy Cats*
Randy F. Nelson, *The Imaginary Lives of Mechanical Men*
Greg Downs, *Spit Baths*
Peter LaSalle, *Tell Borges If You See Him: Tales of Contemporary Somnambulism*
Anne Panning, *Super America*
Margot Singer, *The Pale of Settlement*
Andrew Porter, *The Theory of Light and Matter*
Peter Selgin, *Drowning Lessons*
Geoffrey Becker, *Black Elvis*
Lori Ostlund, *The Bigness of the World*
Linda LeGarde Grover, *The Dance Boots*
Jessica Treadway, *Please Come Back To Me*
Amina Gautier, *At-Risk*
Melinda Moustakis, *Bear Down, Bear North*
E. J. Levy, *Love, in Theory*
Hugh Sheehy, *The Invisibles*
Jacquelin Gorman, *The Viewing Room*
Tom Kealey, *Thieves I've Known*
Karin Lin-Greenberg, *Faulty Predictions*
Monica McFawn, *Bright Shards of Someplace Else*
Toni Graham, *The Suicide Club*
Siamak Vossoughi, *Better Than War*
Lisa Graley, *The Current That Carries*
Anne Raeff, *The Jungle Around Us*